M. ALLYSON SZABO

BLOOD WATER

TAYLOR, MAGE
BOOK TWO

FIRST EDITION

New Hampshire:
Troglodite Services, LLC
July 2020

This is a work of fiction. All the characters and events portrayed in this book are fictional, and any resemblance to real people or incidents is purely coincidental.

BLOOD WATER

First Troglodite printing: July 2020

Published by Troglodite Services, LLC

Jaffrey, NH | info@troglodite.com
Cover design by Starla Huchton, DesignedByStarla.com
Typesetting by Mike Suss

ISBN-13: 9798607199159

Quantity sales. Special discounts are available on quantity purchases by corporations, associations, and others. For details, contact the publisher at the address above.

My Lover

A silver tongue aflame in light,
I watch the river's course.
Through entangled woodlands and deep shade,
Long fingers touch it's source.
Mirror for the sky to see,
ashine, a flood of light.
Colors tremble upon the lips
Of a glossy wave in flight.
Diamond hard and silver bright at moonlight's glance,
Droplets glint upon me.
Blackness enshrouds in Moon's caress,
Cold hands wandering free.
That sylvan flood, my lover is
And never far I roam.
Amongst the reeds and tangled lilies
This river is my home.

—Tracy Panos

This book is dedicated to Lady Laoghaire, the bestest bestie anywhere, ever. Thanks for putting up with my insanity, and encouraging me to work through the mess that's my life. Oh, and I love you, lamp! And to Mikayla, the BEST first editor ever, thanks!

1 – Prelude

The nightlife in Vancouver was always exciting. The inner city was full of restaurants, tourist traps, museums, book stores, and coffee shops, all stacked onto and around one another like interlocking Legos. People streamed in and out of the Granville Island Public Market, through Gastown with its beautiful steam clock, and among the various theaters. Couples strolled the well lit and politely policed paths of Stanley Park, enjoying the pretentious pageant of stars spilling across the sky above. The music of a local band wove its magic among the spreading branches of the massive, gnarled oak tree near the miniature railway.

Farther into the dark recesses of the park lurked more dangerous things, though. They hid away from the lights and the humanity, away from the comforting presence of the uniformed keepers of peace. Hiding among the alleyways and at the docks, skulking among the worst parts of the urban ghetto and the dirtiest corners of the business parks, were beings that lived on blood and fear.

I was one such predator. I was stalking my prey at a popular bar that evening. I watched the frenetic crowd with narrowed, cautious eyes. I skirted the edges of the teeming throng and clung to the shadows, eyes never leaving my quarry. Despite the number of people, I was not noticed, unheard, ignored.

Her hair was the color of maple leaves in autumn, an unparalleled blend of natural reds, oranges and yellows. Looking at her, I could almost smell the autumn bonfire her hair resembled. Her eyes sparkled with attitude and amusement. They promised an internal fire that matched her hair. She was unaware of the silent death that followed her. Her Rubenesque curves clung to the dark grey dress she wore, and her hips swayed from side to side as she made her way off the dance floor and toward the bathrooms. I followed after her, death on silent and invisible feet.

The bathroom door slid shut behind me, its bulk dulling the resonant bass beat to a dull throb. "Great music tonight, eh?" I stepped up to the mirror, fussing with my hair, inspecting her reflection as I did.

Her wine-dark lips curled into a sensual smile, her icy eyes catching my own and holding them for a breath. She broke the gaze then, snapping open her clutch to pull out her makeup. A delicious smirk danced over her features, flirty and inviting. "Yeah, I like the DJ. She's got style." She touched up her lipstick, pursing and smacking her lips together, aware of me as I sized her up.

I moved a step closer to her, mere inches away, but bubbling with a heady tension that we both felt. Her gaze took me in, top to bottom, and then she grinned. She gripped my shoulder with one pale hand, her manicured nails biting into my flesh.

Turning away from the mirror to face her, I reached up and cupped her chin. "You are such a gorgeous woman," I murmured, pulling that full, pouty mouth close enough to kiss. I bit her bottom lip, nibbling at it as we embraced. Where our bodies touched, it felt like molten metal, burning with desire for more. The only sound heard above the background whomp of the music was that of our sloppy kisses.

With an ease born of long practice, I tipped the young woman's head to one side, exposing the ivory curve of her neck. I tongued my fangs as they extended, and sighed happily to myself. I leaned in and bit the exposed flesh, nuzzling all the while.

Tippling from the font, I took only a little of the redhead's precious blood. My sensitive hearing picked up the sound of others approaching the bathroom, and I sighed. Quick and precise, I licked the bite wounds, closing them completely in seconds. I sucked the deep red blood from my own lips before kissing the woman one more time. My hands tangled in her hair, holding her tight, and I savored her flavor and scent before disengaging.

"You are quite sweet, but let's not get caught being naughty in here," I chuckled, as my erstwhile snack attempted to stop me from breaking off the kiss. I brushed a stray autumn-hued strand back into place before scooting out the door as the newcomers entered.

As I exited the bathroom, I almost collided with my lover, Dez. He was a good seven inches taller than me, stocky in build, with a mop of curly, rakish salt and pepper hair on his head. He sported a stylish five o'clock shadow, tinged with the same grey as his hair. I never got bored of looking at his handsome visage.

He steadied me with one hand, and leaned down to kiss me. His nostrils flared and his eyes flashed as he caught the aroma of blood, and he grinned at me.

"Tell me it was the ginger!" he whispered in my ear, his voice eager and breathy. His words tickled at my skin, and I shivered, happy and sated.

"Oh, it was. She's fiery. Hot sauce in her blood." I leaned against Dez, casual and familiar together. I took a deep breath, closing my eyes to process the wide variety of human scents surrounding us. "Did you get the blonde you were after?"

He nodded, pulling me into the milling crowd on the dance floor. "She also was quite the treat," he admitted. "Still, not as striking as yours. Are you almost ready to go home, my dear?" He wrapped one arm around my waist and captured my other hand in his. We swept into a dance move that was wholly inappropriate for the heavy beat the DJ was playing.

"Not on your life!" I followed his lead as he spiraled us around the dance floor like a pro, melting against his strong form. "I'm meeting Clio after this, and we're going to court for a bit, because the Prince wants to see me. Then we're thinking of heading to the business district up in North Van, by Harborview Park. There's some kind of late night rave there."

He nodded, sighing, and his lips quirked up into a grimace. "Magnus gets time with you so rarely, I suppose I shouldn't be jealous. I am, though." His eyes blazed with a dark intensity, and he tightened his grip on my waist, holding me, owning me.

"I like that you're jealous," I admitted. "It makes me feel wanted. In any case, I don't think I'll be home too late. The nights are too short at this time of the year." I pouted.

He nodded. When you were a vampire, dawn was the enemy. You would fall asleep as the sun crested, whether you wanted to or not. If you were stupid enough to be caught outside, you would burn. Summer was the quiet season for us, with long days, and hot, sticky nights that were hours shorter than we wanted. It was springtime now, a few days past the equinox, and our long, languid nights were long gone.

"I'll get some work done in the office, then," he said, and pecked me on the cheek. His lips lingered against my skin longer than necessary, and I drank in the sensation. "See you later." He guided us to the edge of the dance floor before wending his way out of the crowd and the club.

I enjoyed another half hour of sweaty humanity before disengaging from the masses. I left the club, intent on meeting with Clio outside.

Clio was tall, several inches taller than Dez, and very blonde. Her platinum hair cascaded in a silky radiance of soft curls around her oval face. She had very classic looks, with contoured cheeks and wide, crimson lips. She wore a tight white linen skirt and matching sleeveless vest that hung almost to her knees. Her blouse appeared to be made out of gauzy tulle, and left her looking more naked than anything. It was much dressier than her normal pencil skirt and plain blouse, and it was classy as hell. The jacket she was wearing over the entire ensemble was not quite adequate for the current temperature, if you were human. We were not, so it was only for show. I couldn't help staring at her; who could?

Tonight, she appeared to be in 'resting bitch face' mode for some reason, her lips pursed into a thin, dark line. She tapped her toes in staccato in the white strappy stilettos she wore. She was staring at her phone when I approached her, looking aggravated.

"Hi," I ventured, reaching out to touch her arm. "Everything alright?" I swung my distressed leather jacket over my shoulders and slid my arms in. I would look warmer than Clio, but no one would notice me anyhow, standing next to her.

She looked up, startled, and shoved her phone into her purse. "It's fine. I'm on edge. And hungry, as I haven't had time to eat."

"Well, let's go grab a bite then." I pulled one of her arms through mine, and started north along

Davie Street, toward the water. "Do you want to get something right away, or were you planning on doing that after court?"

"Let's just go do court. I have jeans and a shirt with me for after that."

I raised one eyebrow. "You, in jeans? Since when?"

"I'm trying something different," she stated, her voice terse. "Magnus is buried in paperwork right now, and we haven't had a lot of time for fun. So I'm attempting to find fun without him." Her long, luscious legs were speeding up as she talked, the click of her heels against the pavement punctuating her words. "Which I will succeed at," she stated through clenched teeth.

"Girlfriend, you need to slow down." I tugged her out of her speedy walk and into a saunter. "We'll have fun tonight, and yes you'll succeed. And we'll have some yummy beach food, too, and dance like fools for half the night."

She squeezed my arm, grip tight. "Thank you. I have not been dealing well with the current stress in the city. Even when Magnus is around, he's not really mentally with me, if that makes sense."

"It does. Dez gets that way, too, when he's balls deep in some mathematical formula. As you know." Clio, being Dez's sometimes-assistant within the Sanguinem, was well aware of his ability to disappear so much into work that he forgot to eat.

"I do know. I know that 'hangry' vampires are bad vampires."

I grinned up at Clio, and we made our way along the dark, quiet streets toward where I had parked my car. The noise and chaos of the bar district faded behind us, and we moved into a more residential area. Recently gentrified, the condominiums and apartments were clean and sleek, rising up into the dark night sky. The Stanley Park seawall stretched ahead of us, and we strolled along it, controlling our gait. Both of us were capable of moving at a pace much faster than the average human, but the point was to blend in.

Of course, Clio didn't blend in anywhere. Her tall and stately form stood out from a mile off, and when you added the high heels and sheer linen, it didn't help. I was a mere shadow beside her. I didn't mind, though. My days of being jealous of Clio were long over. I had my own skill set, and it rivaled her own. We didn't compete; we teamed up. I'm told it's terrifying to behold.

I spied a small group of young men ahead, where the seawall jutted in to avoid a tide pool surrounded by a miniature sandy beach. During daylight hours, mothers would bring their little ones to play there, protected from the waves of English Bay. Now, in the deep of night, another type of play was going on.

I licked my lips, noting the female the eight or so men were pushing back and forth between them. She cowered, shivering, her hazel eyes flicking from one man to another in panic. Her face was pale, almost as pale as my own, and her hands were clenched tight at her side. Her entire body was strung tight like a bowstring, as she snatched for the coat being held by one of the miscreants. I nudged Clio, jarring her from her private thoughts, and indicated the scene.

We approached at a slow pace, lazy smiles on our faces. The girl's eyes met my own, a pleading look in them but also a warning, an unspoken message to run away while we could. Tonight was her lucky night, though. I saw no reason to run; these little boys posed no threat to me, and they wouldn't be harming her any further this evening, either.

"Good evening, gentlemen," Clio purred, that cultured voice of hers alluring, soft, beckoning. They turned to us as one, and jostled each other as they stared. I doubt they were used to being inspected by women, and even moreso at night. "I don't suppose you'd like to provide us with some entertainment, would you?"

I stopped myself from chuckling. Clio could be a real bitch when she wanted to, and I suspected she was about to take out her frustration with city tensions on these miscreants. I walked up to the male holding the girl's wrist and coat, and deftly released her, holding his own wrist in my hand instead.

"You like to frighten women?" I inquired in a soft and dangerous tone. My grip tightened, and I could feel the fragile bones shift, and hear the sharp indrawn breath of pain from him. I stopped before I broke anything. Barely. I retrieved the girl's coat and tossed it to her.

"What's it to you?" One of the men stepped out from the pack, separating himself from his fellows, outing himself as a leader. Others shuffled behind him, uncomfortable but not willing to stand up. The one I was holding tried to pull away, but discovered that my hand was rather like a manacle. The whites of his eyes showed, fear enveloping him. I could smell the rank sweat of him as he realized that he did not have the upper hand.

I tapped the young woman's shoulder, and gestured toward the well lit, patrolled streets farther up. "Go on. Escape while you can." She paused less than a second before tearing off at top speed, not bothering to slide into her coat or even look back.

Leader boy looked as if he was going to protest, but then fell silent as Clio's full force of personality focused on him. Clio's talents included a type of mesmerism. She could command a room full of humans by doing nothing more than demanding their attention. Eight human males, already off balance and intoxicated, were no test of her prowess. Even my own prey was focused on her, fully engaged, ignoring me despite my iron grip on his wrist. I grinned, and watched it play out.

Clio stroked the leader's cheek, then grasped his chin roughly in her hands. For a moment, I thought she might drink from him right there. I scanned the area, poignantly aware of the throngs of humanity wandering only a few blocks away. I couldn't hear any vehicles closer than that, though. Across the street were several apartment buildings, all with big, glass windows overlooking the bay. This was not a good place for indulging. Clio had also realized that, though, and took the hand of the young man in front of her. The group of us walked away, silent and focused, up the seawall toward the rocky beaches at the outskirts of Stanley Park.

As we reached the cover of thickets of trees, Clio eased the entire group into the shadows. I still had the wrist of my own prey, and I pushed him past a dark bush and into an area likely used for late night sexual trysts. I didn't have Clio's ability to control the minds of my victims, but he was already pliable and afraid. I lifted his arm up, fingers caressing the soft skin on the wrist where all the veins could be seen. He made a single attempt to pull away, a tiny whimper escaping from his chest, and then gave in as I leaned in to bite. I held his eyes as I suckled at the hot, iron spring, revelling at the life force I was taking. After several heady mouthfuls, I licked and closed the wound.

I showed him his healed wrist, and leaned in to speak in a voice so soft it was not more than a whisper. "You won't die. You won't even suffer, really, at least on a physical level. But you're going to leave young ladies alone now, aren't you?" He nodded stiffly, unable to move due to his terror. I'm sure his wrist was still smarting. I could have fed in a way that caused him to feel nothing. Biting him as I did was cruel and somewhat painful, and I'd meant it to be. I didn't like bullies. I didn't like them at all.

I wiped the last of his blood from the corner of my mouth, and held it between my fingers. I rubbed them together, feeling it slick and warm there. His eyes followed the motion as he tried not to pant or whimper. I closed my eyes, concentrating momentarily. A little tweak here and there, and I used his blood to alter his memory of the entire situation. He would remember the girl, trapping her among them, and then a sense of pain and unease, and fear. I left the fear alone. Let him stew in that for a while.

When I finished with my erstwhile criminal, I looked over at Clio. She had caused several of the men to sleep, and was finishing up with the two she'd chosen to snack on. Amazingly, her white linen was still crisp and pristine despite laying in a bush and sipping blood. She amazed me with her ability to always be perfect. Looking down at myself, I discovered a couple of droplets here and there, which I hastily cleaned up, sighing to myself. Klutzy to the core.

Standing, I brushed leaf litter off myself. "Ready to go?" I asked. Clio rose on those gazelle like legs of hers, white and delicate despite her height.

"I am," she conceded. "I feel better. Thank you."

"My pleasure," I smiled. "I always feel better after spanking bad boys, don't you?"

Sticking to the shadows and uninhabited areas, we moved away from our stunned and fallen prey. We took alleys and back streets at a speed that would seem unreal to a human, returning to my car.

It bleeped happily at us as I approached it and pushed the key fob button. I slid behind the wheel and latched my seat belt, waiting for Clio to do the same.

"Straight to court now?" I asked.

"I think so, Alexandra. Let's get this over with."

❧❦

I sped along the local highway, making a beeline for Annacis Island. As we went over the bridge, I mused over how different this trip was today as opposed to the first time I'd been here. I had been human then, a living and breathing person with a life. Now, I had no heartbeat and didn't need to breathe, and yet I was more alive than I'd ever been. I had a place here. I knew the route so well that I didn't think about it anymore when I drove it. It was second nature.

The BC Fisheries building was as boring as ever. I parked in my usual spot, near a tree and a light. I didn't need the light, but old habits die hard. I'd needed streetlights for far longer than I'd been able to see in the dark. Clio and I entered the glass front doors and nodded to the receptionist. We headed down the left corridor to the elevator, not pausing to talk to anyone.

"Do we have anything in particular we're doing tonight?" I asked as the doors slid closed and Clio put her key into the lock that allowed us to go straight to the top floor.

"No, but Magnus wanted everyone to check in this week. He's doing his best to keep tabs on things right now." Clio shrugged, her shoulders rippling under the thin material of her shirt. "I think he just likes to talk to you, to be honest, though he is touching base with everyone."

"I like him, too," I admitted. And I did. Of all the vampires I knew in Vancouver and abroad, Magnus was one of my favorites. He was a good choice as Prince of the city, as well, because he had no illusions that he was better than anyone else. He happened to be more skilled at herding cats, which made him an excellent administrator.

The throne room doors were closed, and I examined them in detail as we sat on the bench chatting. A hoard of skeletal bodies was attacking, pillaging, and raping a village full of fresh faced, plump human beings. Some of the humans were running in fear, while others seemed oblivious to the army of death among them. No matter how often I sat there staring, I always found some new perversion that I hadn't seen before. Tonight was no different.

Clio was talking about what Magnus was studying lately, when the big doors slid open. I hadn't been paying attention to her, and I lost track completely as a very large, very smelly being left the throne room. My nose crinkled in self-defense, and I forced myself to stop breathing, in sheer self defense.

It was like being attacked by a sheepdog that had come in from a ten mile hike in the rain. Gah!

Clio's mouth fell open and her sentence trailed off, forgotten. She stared in a very not-Clio-like way. His heartbeat was hot and fast, and there was no question he was male, but was most definitely not human. Everyone in the hallway gawked as he walked away, oblivious to us. When he had disappeared around the corner, everything came to life once more.

"What the hell was that?" I demanded, as Clio blurted out, "Oh my lord, that was a werewolf!" Her hand fluttered to her mouth, a motion that belonged more in a silent movie than a modern hallway.

I stared at her. "Werewolf. As in hairy, turns into a dog at the full moon, howls at night, eats people, werewolf?" I made a point of taking a deep breath, painful as that was. I committed that scent to memory, in case I ever came across it again. Still, I'd been all over Vancouver, and I'd never run into anything like it before. I would remember the intensity, if not the stench of it. It defied forgetting.

"I think so." She stood and darted into the throne room. I followed, human conventions and speeds abandoned. She dropped to one knee before her lord, shaken and falling back on protocol. Magnus managed to straighten out the upset look on his face, then smiled at her and took her hand.

"Come sit here, darling. And Alexandra, you too." He crooked a finger at me, and I approached the dais with deference. Magnus was the Prince of

Vancouver, and friend or not, I always acted with great respect toward him. He had earned it. We both ascended, and settled into the chairs brought for us.

"Was that what I think it was?" Clio demanded, brow furrowed with worry.

"He was. Don't refer to him as 'it', Clio. Rokku and his kind live in the woods and northern areas where we don't penetrate. There have been disturbances up there, where his people generally live."

"What kind of disturbances?" I tried to think of anything that would bother a community of whatever his people were. If they were all as large and burly as he, anything short of rabid grizzlies likely wasn't much of a problem.

"We aren't certain. They've found bodies drained of blood, however."

"Vampires eat werewolves? Isn't there some kind of thing about not doing that, or is that a fictional thing?" I tried to imagine sucking blood out of him. The thought of the smell alone was enough to make me gag. I couldn't bring myself to give serious thought to eating it, even if he did have a hot, throbby attraction to him.

"No!" Magnus said, aghast. "Heavens no. You must have smelled him. They are... not human enough to pass, for the most part. They live up on the Native lands, often in areas no one else will go to. They're self sufficient, and they stay in secluded areas. They don't interact much with humans, for obvious reasons. We don't interact much with them, either. And no, we definitely don't eat them. They're not at all edible, from our point of view."

They weren't edible from anything's point of view, I thought to myself, shaking my head. "So what's killing them, then?" I was curious what this had to do with the vampire community. When Magnus said they didn't "pass", he meant pass as human, and I agreed. Perhaps in a dark alley, away from all light and after taking away someone's glasses, he might pass as human. Barely. Upwind.

"We don't know. They don't know. They came to us after they used up all their own resources, because we're much in control of the night life. I had nothing for him, though. We'll offer what help we can. Like us, they are creatures of darkness and night. They are misunderstood and maligned based on legends and stories rather than reality."

I nodded, thoughtful. What would hunt werewolves? I mean, these were hulking, humanesque things. I shuddered a bit. It was kind of terrifying to think that they had an enemy. I wondered what it was. I was sure I didn't want to run into it.

Magnus waved away the mental clutter, and asked me a few questions about Dez and the Sanguinem. I answered him as best I could. Being a junior member of the family meant I didn't know all that much. Being Dez's lover meant people expected me to know more than I did. It was a crappy situation to be in, but it was what it was.

Business being dealt with, I headed out. Clio stayed behind, hoping to catch a few minutes of time with Magnus, was my guess. I decided to go to Ambleside Beach to walk and hunt, near the place where I'd been earlier with Clio.

The original males had dissipated into the dark night. A hardy group of young people were partying and smoking there. I spent a while dancing and milling amongst the drunk and drug-hazed humans there, but my heart wasn't in it. I couldn't help thinking about the werewolf, and what could hunt something that size. It was disturbing!

In the wee hours, not long before dawn, I headed back to my car. I had parked along the railway tracks this time, away from the beaches and the lights. I trudged along at human speed, slow and as normal as I could manage. I was too aware of late night dog walkers and passionate couples lurking in the shadows to use my more-than-human speed. And that's where I ran across the body.

2 – Oh Crap...

I looked at the corpse at my feet critically. I was sad he was dead, yes. It was a melancholy thing, and I really felt for him. But he was dead, not alive, and now I had a corpse at my feet. Stop looking at me like that, by the way. I didn't kill him, I found him like this.

Well, at least there was blood. Being a blood mage meant I could do magic with blood. Having no skill at math meant I sucked at learning the blood magic formulas I should have. Instead, I tended to wing it. Admittedly, that meant a lot of trial and error, with a high degree of error involved. Still, I did get things done.

I wondered what happened when you used corpse's blood for magic. No time like the present to find out, right? I flipped out a vial from my jacket pocket, and scooped up some of the blood from one of the many gaping wounds on the corpse.

Holding the vial between my hands, I closed my eyes and concentrated. The question was, what did I want to do? Well, how about I figure out who killed the corpse? I wasn't sure if it was supernatural or human in nature, so that might be a good place to begin. I focused all my energy on the vial of blood, willing it to present me with answers.

"It was a woman," came a raspy voice from my feet. I jerked, startled, and the tiny glass vial fell to the ground and shattered, sending glowing droplets of blood spattering across the pavement. "I don't know her," the corpse continued, the voice rumbling and low. "But she was naked as a jaybird…" It sat up, and upon examining its own body, it began to sob.

Well crap…

⤳⤳

Half an hour later, I had made no further progress on figuring out how to undo what I had done. Still, the corpse was no longer crying. That was a blessing. It's hard to think of something more disturbing than having a dead man crying at your feet. Why was this happening to me? Why hadn't Dez warned me about this? I understand he couldn't anticipate every little thing I might do, but I was having a hard time wondering why he wouldn't warn me about not raising the dead!

I did not want to bring this home with me. Dez was going to be unhappy. I was already painfully aware that his ire was going to be high. Damn it! What choice did I have, though? This wasn't the kind of thing I could call Clio about, and Magnus was right out. I couldn't leave it here, either, because Dead Man Walking was not kosher in Vancouver. Dez was my only reasonable choice.

I crouched down beside the animated corpse, doing my best to look calm and relaxed. I failed miserably. I felt awkward about this entire scenario. "Hi. I'm Alexandra. Can you tell me your name?"

He looked up at me, having been staring at his rather bloated hands. "I'm James. Jim. Everyone calls me Jim." I could understand him, without difficulty, but his words were muffled, as if he had cotton in his mouth. A sense of dread crept over me as I realized his tongue must be swollen.

"Alright Jim, that's good. Are you… in any pain?" I struggled to find appropriate questions to ask. What did one ask a corpse? I was in the dark on this one.

"I don't really feel anything." He shook his head, as if trying to clear away cobwebs. "I don't remember anything. No, that's not true. I remember the girl. She was beautiful." He trailed off. He looked at his torso, and my own eyes followed.

It was obvious he had been stabbed several times. There were holes in his blood soaked clothing, and presumably in the flesh underneath. His fingers traced the wound tracks as if he were a toddler finger painting. It was a rather gruesome image no matter how you looked at it.

"I'm glad you aren't hurting, Jim. That's a good thing." I think, I muttered to myself, unwilling to voice my lack of knowledge. "However, we can't have you lying here. That would not be good. Someone might see us, and I have a feeling that we would both be in a lot of trouble. So upsy daisy, we're going to go to my car." I helped Jim to his feet.

Explaining this to Dez was going to be a treat. I was pretty sure he was going to be pissed and upset. I also figured he was going to be unhappy about having a corpse in the house. It wasn't like I could just leave him laying around, though.

Then a new thought hit me. Maybe this was a part of the creation of a vampire! When I'd woken up after being turned, I was whole and perfect. But I knew from listening to the story of it that I had been mortally injured in a car accident. Perhaps Jim here had been turned into a vampire, but hadn't yet completed the process? Why the hell hadn't I asked Dez about this before? It hadn't even occurred to me to ask him how vampires were made. You'd think that would be one of the first questions I asked myself. I got angry, with myself and with Dez.

"Jim, I'm going to need you to act natural," I stated, taking off my jacket and draping it around his shoulders. At least his head was all in one piece. The jacket covered the worst of the damage, though it didn't do much to hide the blood saturating his trousers. They were dark colored and it was that "dark before the dawn" moment of night when everything was silent. It would have to do. I looked up and down the sea wall path, which was well lit and paved. I couldn't see my car, but knew it was a little along the tracks and beyond the tree line. There shouldn't be any video cameras or people there. It was a quiet road even at busy times.

I hustled Jim down the path and across the railroad tracks, then hastened across the road to my vehicle. I opened the back door and shoved him in unceremoniously. "Buckle up, buttercup," I muttered, and hopped into the driver's seat in front of him.

I paused, and took a deep, cleansing breath. Tearing off into the black night at top speed felt like it was the right thing to do, but it would bring attention to myself. The very last thing I wanted tonight was to be stopped by an overzealous cop bent on doing good. I pulled out of my parking space with a calm I did not feel, and stuck to the speed limit the entire drive home.

Every stoplight and every slow down caused me to tighten my hands on the steering wheel. I thought about calling Dez, talking to him while I drove, but I decided against that. Better to get his mad all over with at once. I took the time to text him to meet me in the garage, though, as I didn't want to park outside.

"You okay back there, Jim?" I peeked back at him via my rear view mirror. He was looking out the window, a bemused expression on his face. His bloody fingers traced a pattern on the cool glass.

"I think that I might be dead," he said, his voice so faint I almost didn't hear him. "I have… holes."

"Let's not dwell on that." I spoke with a strength I didn't feel, and picked a different conversational direction to go in. "You said the girl who attacked you was naked. Where did she come from?" I'd found him on the cement path on the river, between the beach area I'd been dancing at, and my car. Had the girl been at the party? Several of the women had wandered off into the bushes to engage in a little fun with the males, but none had been naked. Was it another vampire? I hadn't smelled anything. I hadn't noticed any marks on the people at the party, indicating they'd been fed on by other vampires.

Fifteen minutes of driving had never seemed so long. I steeled myself at each traffic signal, hoping beyond hope to get home before someone looked into the back of my car. I know humans are often lacking in sense, and don't look much beyond the end of their nose. I was counting on their lack of observational skills.

I breathed a heavy sigh of relief as I pulled up the long driveway to Sanguinem House. My lovely home opened out before me, full of light. The garage door was open, and I pulled into the cavernous space. I hit the door closer, and sat there, hands glued to the steering wheel, until it trundled shut behind me. I just about went through the windshield when Dez knocked at my window. I caught myself hissing at him, a habit I disliked in myself.

"Geezus, love, don't do that!" I got out of the car and flung myself into his arms. "I am so glad you're here."

"Where else would I be?" he asked, kissing the top of my head. "Now what's going on? And what's that smell?" He sniffed at me, then at my car. I wondered if he was picking up the scent of werewolf or corpse.

"Dez, this is Jim," I stated in a bland tone, opening the door. Jim, for his part, sat there staring at us. His blood stained clothing hung around him, making a mess of my leather seats.

Dez started to say something several times, and stopped himself. His nostrils flared, and he lifted up a single finger as if about to make a point, then dropped it again. Finally, he broke out with, "I don't know what to say."

"Pleased to meet you," said Jim, raising a filthy, bloated hand that shook as if he were shivering. "I think I'm dead."

Dez looked from the dead man to me and back again. "Alexandra." It wasn't a question. I wasn't even sure it was a statement. It sounded more like an accusation, for all that he used a soft, even tone.

"I didn't know what to do with him."

"Well it's obvious you did something with him, Alexandra." His voice was strangled, and very quiet. "Otherwise he'd be wherever he was when you found him. Tell me, was he alive when you found him? Did you kill him?" His voice went from angry to puzzled. He knew me as a generally kind person, not prone to insane stabbings in back alleys.

"I found him d-" I stopped myself. "Can we get him in the house and let him clean up a bit, while I talk to you alone? Please, Dez?"

Jim didn't respond to our talking about him or around him. He just watched us go back and forth, silent and oozing. Dez rubbed his temples, looking tired.

"I'll get one of my people to come deal with this. And then we'll talk." He turned on a heel and strode out of the garage. I winced, feeling the anger coming off him in waves.

"Up you get, Jim." I helped the man to his feet. "Do you think you can shower? I'm pretty sure we've got some clothing you can wear."

"I think so," he said. He was steadier now, standing on his own. He looked a lot less stunned than he had earlier. I wondered again if I was actually witnessing someone turning into a vampire. The holes in his chest were not healing. They were, however, bubbling. They continued to ooze a combination of blood and other liquids.

The minions arrived, taking charge of Jim and the car clean up. I found myself wondering how I'd managed, living without servants before my death. They did so much for us.

I went out of the garage, through the causeway, into the house and through the kitchen's back door. I made my way to Dez's office on the lower level of our home. He was pacing back and forth, looking for all the world like a bomb about to go off. A vampiric bomb.

"Alexandra, I need you to explain exactly what led you to bringing that… thing home." He motioned me to sit at his desk, and I slid into the hard wooden chair, curling in on myself, arms crossed. I related the whole tale, including the blood magic I'd done. His eyes widened, and then a pained look crossed his face. He rubbed one hand over his forehead as if attempting to smooth the furrows there.

"Is he becoming a vampire?" I asked. "Dez, did I accidentally do to him what you did to me, to bring me back?"

"No, Alex. No you did not. You have animated a corpse. Except you should not have been able to do that. And why would you even think about doing it? What possessed you to play with dead blood?" His voice rose until this last was almost a shout. I cringed back, looking down.

"I don't know what I can and cannot do, Dez. You know that! I can do all sorts of odd crap without breaking a sweat, and you claim it's hard. And your easy stuff is almost impossible for me. I don't know! So I experiment. I ran across a body and figured I'd find out who killed the guy. The result was… that!" I flung my arm in the direction of the bathroom.

"It didn't occur to you that perhaps doing magic with the blood of a dead thing was bad?" he asked, sarcasm heavy in his voice. His lips had pressed together into a caricature of a smile.

"Well, no, hon. If you hadn't noticed, WE are dead. I didn't make the distinction." My voice rose as a response to his, and I sounded shrill and angry. This was hardly my fault! I mean, well, it was my fault, but not really my fault. My brain spasmed under the strain of that last thought.

He sighed, and lowered himself into the antique office chair beside me. "Well, here's one for you. We do not play with the blood of dead-but-inanimate things. Ever. It's forbidden."

It was my turn to look confused. "Why not? And didn't you do so when you made me?"

"It's not the same thing, Alexandra. And I had to get permission for that."

"Well, only sort of. You asked forgiveness rather than permission, remember."

"Yes, well." He rubbed the bridge of his nose, and I noted again how very tired he was looking. I felt a pit of sadness, knowing I was part of the reason behind his weariness.

Being the head of the Sanguinem was sometimes easy, but often exhausting labor. We'd had an influx of household members lately, and several were being hosted in our home. Others were at nearby safe houses, and paperwork and safeties had to be put in place for every one. Court had been complex, and sometimes unsavory. Hunting lands had been redefined due to a new enclave in the mountains to the north of the city. Everything was taking its toll. I thought back to Clio and her frustration with Magnus, and realized our discomfort came from the same source. Growth and expansion was never easy. Even for immortal creatures of the night, it was disturbing.

"What you've done is not the creation of vampiric life, my love. That is done in a very specific way unrelated to what you did. Your actions can only be described as necromantic."

"Necromantic. I thought all our love was necromantic," I quipped nervously.

Dez groaned at my terrible pun. "Necromancy is the practice of raising the dead, animating them. That is what you have done. Jim is not a vampire, and the sustaining force that keeps us whole and hale is not coursing through his veins. You can tell, because his wounds are not healing. He's decaying. That's what the smell is."

"Ew." I thought about that. "So we can do necromancy, too? You didn't think to mention this to me?"

"No, Alexandra, we can't. And this is a bad thing. I don't know how you managed to do this."

"Me either, Dez. And I didn't do it to irritate you. I figured I'd learn something new. I try to do that on a regular basis."

"I know, love. I know." He reached up to stroke my cheek, struggling to hide the upset and sadness lurking in his dark eyes. "I have to call Magnus, though. And we'll need to question your corpse. And then I'll need you to reverse your magic and put it back to rest. We can't allow a decaying corpse to wander the area, and it's not staying here."

"Won't he just decay into nothing, at some point?"

"I don't know, Alex. Sometimes magic can halt the decay. It's obvious that either he was dead for a while before you found him, or that the decay has continued."

"He said he was murdered by a girl," I offered.

"I doubt a girl could have killed him. Not a human one, at least. His chest was punctured quite deep, from what I could see. I suppose we'll have to investigate, though. More work. Always more work."

Aubrey, one of the human women who 'interned' (for lack of a better word) for Dez at night, appeared at the office door. I could hear the quiet thump-thump of her heartbeat, though she seemed quite calm. "It- He is clean now, and I put him in the safe room," she said. "The shower seems to have taken care of the worst of the smell, but he isn't healing. And I have someone cleaning the shower now."

"Thanks Aubrey," Dez replied. "We'll be there in a few minutes. Make sure he's not able to wander off, please." She nodded and disappeared.

"I'll go get him settled for the day," I offered. "You call Magnus. It's too close to dawn to deal with this right now, but come tomorrow evening, I'll do whatever needs doing." I wanted nothing more than to take this off his plate, to solve my own problems. It never seemed to work that way, though.

Dez nodded, and picked up his cell from the desktop. I slipped out of the office and along the hallway to the heavy steel security door that led to our safe room. Aubrey opened the door for me and I entered. Jim was there, clean and dressed in a pair of track pants and a tee shirt. He didn't look so bad, now that the blood had been washed away. He was attempting to comb his hair, though his grip on the comb was not great. His dexterity was definitely lacking, and he was puffy all over.

"Hi again," I ventured. "How are you doing?"

"I'm alright, I suppose. As alright as I can be while being dead. I'm pretty sure I'm dead. I don't have a heartbeat. And I have holes in my chest. And they aren't bleeding." He ran one swollen hand over the front of his shirt, a nervous gesture.

"Yes, you're dead." I wasn't sure how to put that in polite terms, and he'd figured it out on his own anyhow. The stab marks sort of gave it away.

He nodded. "You're also dead. No heartbeat."

It was my turn to nod. "Correct. But we are not undead in the same way." This was one of the most bizarre conversations I'd had, and that was saying something.

"You seem healthy. I'm not." He was quite observant for a corpse. "I don't feel bad, though. I don't feel anything at all, to be honest."

"I'm sorry about this. I'm not sure what's happened. Dez, the man that I talked to earlier, is going to call some experts. I hope they will be able to come up with answers."

"I see." He paused for a moment, then met my eyes. His own were still bright, not yet glazed over. I wondered if the corneas would cloud while he was animate. I shuddered as he continued. "You have experts on walking dead people?"

I chuckled under my breath, because the other option was to cry, and I wasn't going to do that. "Only sort of. Dez seems to have some clue as to what happened, although I don't understand most of it myself. I guess I've done some sort of forbidden magic. I didn't realize it, though. My own magic is so different from everyone else's that it's hard to come up with a set of rules that applies to me."

"So we're not alike. What are you?" He seemed genuinely curious. Leaving aside the slight scent of death that hung around him, he was a personable fellow. I felt bad for him. He was taking the whole thing rather well, all things considered.

"I'm a vampire, undead," I replied. "Current theories posit that we're animated by a virus or bacteria of some sort. We haven't done a lot of scientific research into the whole thing, yet, though. We don't tend to turn scientists."

He nodded, a thoughtful look on his face. "And me?"

"I don't know. That's what I'm hoping Dez and others will be able to tell us about. There are others who are much older than I am, who have more expertise, and more knowledge."

The heavy door slid open with a hiss, and Dez entered. The corners of his usually smiling mouth were pulled down, and his forehead was wrinkled. I sighed softly to myself, knowing the signs of stress in him. It was my fault, which made it all that much worse. I hated myself, right that moment.

Dez walked right past me without a glance, and over to Jim. "I'm afraid you're going to have to stay with us for a while. What Alexandra has done is inexcusable and will be punished. Until we figure out how to remedy this situation, we cannot allow you to leave."

Jim shrugged. "Okay. Not sure where I'd go. I'm not looking well at the moment. Gaping chest wounds, and such."

Dez frowned. "Yes, your body is in decay. I'm going to be very blunt with you, because I can't afford not to be. You're not only dead, you're dead and animated. The force that sustains us, and some other supernatural creatures, is missing from you. I don't know when your body will decompose. I don't know if the decomposition we're seeing at present began before Alexandra's inexperienced meddling. You may be suspended like this, or you may continue to degrade. However, it appears to me that your consciousness is now linked to your body, alive or not. We have some elders who will be coming over tomorrow evening to talk to you and Alexandra. We hope to figure things out. Until then, you'll be held in this room."

Jim listened to Dez's diatribe without flinching. He nodded here and there. "Do you have any books, maybe? I don't feel like I can sleep. I'd like to have something to do today." He seemed completely unshaken by everything, unphased by being dead, having stab wounds, the bloating. I shifted from foot to foot, watching uneasily.

"You can read. Ask Alexandra to fetch you a book or three. She'll be happy to help you out. Do you want food or drink?" I doubt Jim noticed the intensity in Dez's eyes as he asked this, but I did. The answer was important to him.

"No, I don't feel hungry or thirsty. Just… bored." Jim shrugged once more.

"Good enough. Goodnight, Jim. It was nice meeting you. I wish it had been under better circumstances." Dez nodded at me as he strode out, closing the door behind him.

"I am afraid I need to go, too," I murmured. "It's close to dawn, and I need to sleep. Will you be alright? What kind of books do you like?"

"I don't know what I like. Science fiction maybe?"

I fetched down some Time Enough for Love by Heinlein, the first Dune book by Herbert, and a handful of pulp fiction. Once Jim was settled and had a cot set up should he feel the need to sleep, I slipped out and locked the heavy door behind me.

I showered as quick as I could, scouring away the lingering stench of death that still clung to me from the car trip. After towel drying my hair, I made my way to Dez's bedroom. Our bedroom. The door was closed, so I knocked.

"Enter," he called out in a quiet voice. I pushed open the door, and saw him standing at the end of the bed. He was still dressed, and he looked exhausted and stressed.

"I'm sorry," I began. My stomach had dropped, leaving me feeling queasy over the whole thing. I hated fighting with Dez. My relationship with him was vastly important to me, although it was much healthier than past ones I'd had. I could survive without him, and had a life of my own, but I didn't like it when we were fighting.

"I'm sorry too, Alex. You're right. You couldn't have known there were issues with using dead blood. It didn't even occur to me to say anything. It's so ground into us that it didn't seem to need saying. Magnus is beyond angry at the moment. Clio and he will be over tomorrow evening. I'm not sure who else he's bringing. We will deal."

I sidled over and nuzzled myself into his arms, my cheek against his shoulder. "I wish we didn't have to. I had no idea this would happen." I fought back the tears I felt welling up in my eyes, willing them to go away. Cleaning up blood tears sucked, and I didn't want to have to do that on top of everything else.

Dez stripped down to his boxers, tossing his dirty clothing into the hamper. I watched this normal, every-day motion with a kind of silent awe. We were dead, vampires, mythical creatures of the night. Yet we still got undressed for bed, and we still did laundry. It was strange and amazing, and a lot weird. Even after more than a year of it, I still found it difficult to fathom, some days.

He looked up at me, and smiled, his face soft and gentle. It was a tired smile, but a real one. He settled onto the end of the bed, and patted it. I joined him, pressing close to him once more. "Can you tell me what exactly led to the current situation?" he asked. "It might help if I understood the minutia."

I went over the process of finding the body and focusing on the blood. Unfortunately, this was always where our conversations broke down.

"You just 'felt' the blood?" He sounded exasperated.

"Yes," I said. "I closed my eyes, and I reached out for it with my... my center? My energy? I don't know how to describe it. And once I felt it and had it in my mental grasp, I thought my question at it."

"And what was this question?"

I thought back to the moment when the blood was in the vial, and Jim was at my feet. "I was thinking it would be good to know who'd killed the corpse," I replied. "And I was not sure if he'd been murdered by one of us, or by another human. And then instead of the answer popping into my head, like I expected, or a glowing trail to appear, he just answered."

"You are definitely not supposed to be able to 'just do that', Alex. We don't practice necromancy anymore because it was used for some horrific things in the far past. Clio will be able to tell you more about the abuses of the necromancers. They were a family like ours, and connected to ours. But because of their actions, they were hunted down and eradicated. Every last one was destroyed."

"You all killed an entire family?" I asked, aghast.

He nodded. "We did. It was necessary, as I understand it."

"So what does this mean? About me, I mean?"

"I don't know, hon." His shoulders sagged.

"Am I not a member of the Sanguinem, then? Am I a necromancer? Or is it like we're blood mages but we're members of the Sanguinem, and there's another name for what I am?" My voice shook as I felt the edges of my universe wavering. For the past year or so, everything had been just right. I knew what I was, and my world had fallen into place. And now, in the space of three hours, all that seemed to be slipping away.

"I don't know. I am hoping Magnus or Clio will be able to explain more to us tomorrow. They are going to come here, rather than risk us transporting Jim to them."

I nodded. "Will I have to leave here if I'm not a member of the Sanguinem anymore?"

He started to answer, then stopped. Then he grabbed me up in one of his lovely bear hugs. "I have no idea what happened in the past, but in the modern world, a lot of those traditions have been abandoned. I don't care what family you're a part of. You are in my life, and I'm not letting go. It may be that you're the start of a new bloodline, and that's fine. You can still live here. WE can still live here."

I buried my face in his chest, taking a deep breath in, enjoying his scent. The fear kept gnawing at me, though. "If I'm a necromancer, does that mean they'll put me down? Kill me?" Having come to terms with eternal unlife, I wasn't willing to give it up. I didn't want to die.

"They would have to come through me first," he growled, his grip on my arms tightening. "And that is not an idle threat. No one will take you from me."

3 – History Lessons

Clio and Magnus settled onto our couch. Anselem had come with them, poncy and stuck up as ever. He was well versed in history, though, and knew more about our past than many. Dez stood off to one side, and I sat on the stone plinth of the fireplace, enjoying the heat of the fire on my back.

"This is not something we can brush under the rug" Magnus began. "There are reasons the necromancers were executed to a man."

Clio nodded, her shoulders sagging, her eyes downcast. She avoided looking at me. "They did many horrible things. The last of them was exterminated in the late 1600s. They are the reason behind many of the myths of people coming back from the dead. Vampires have always managed to hide from or among the humans. These animated corpses, these zombies, have no such sense of self preservation. They can walk during the day, when we cannot. They continue to rot, although at a much retarded pace than an inanimate corpse. What is worse is that their consciousness is usually tied to their rotting bodies. They continue to be aware, even after they decompose beyond movement or interaction with the world. Unlike ghosts, they are unable to move or leave their body. They are tied to that physical body, as if they still inhabit it."

Dez listened without speaking, and I played with the edge of my shirt as they talked.

Magnus nodded. "The horrors of the Renaissance necromancers were beyond compare. If a human caused them trouble, they would kill them and then raise them from the dead. They maintained rigid control over the walking corpse, which they would then bury. Imagine being trapped in a coffin, rotting away over time, unable to move. Imagine being aware of the decomposition of your own body. Imagine being conscious as some unknowing human mummified you or otherwise prepared you for burial. It was awful."

Clio smoothed the already clean lines of her skirt. "The necromancers didn't terrorize only humans, either. Because their creations could day walk, they would send them to do things while the rest of us slept. They could make their minions slaughter other vampires in their sleep. And you know some of us take human companions, Alexandra. Think how it would be, to see your lovely human lover killed, raised, and forced to do horrible things to you. We cannot stress the extreme nature of those who were exterminated."

"But Dez told me they were all slaughtered. You said it just now, Clio. How can I have done this thing if I'm not a member of that family?"

"The Immortuos, as they were called then, were completely destroyed. But all families come about because of spontaneous mutation. It's possible you are one of those mutations." Magnus spoke in a low voice, but his body was stiff.

"We're not suggesting you will be destroyed, Alexandra," Clio said, patting my knee.

"I would hope to hell not!" Dez broke out of his silence. "I am as horrified by this turn of events as you are, but this is hardly her fault. She had no idea this would happen. If anything, it is my fault for not telling her to leave dead blood alone. It didn't occur to me that I'd have to tell anyone that, after all. Dead blood has been useless to vampires for over 400 years."

"Be calm, Hades," Magnus said. "No one is destroying anyone. The Immortuos were exterminated back then was because they were immoral and evil. Alexandra is neither immoral nor evil. Hence this part is not a problem. However, it may be that we must render you unable to create progeny, Alex." He finally looked at me, meeting my eyes and sighing.

"Considering I have no idea how it's done, and have no interest in doing so, I may consent to that." Better than being offed, I thought to myself. I mean, hm… death or having no kids? Yeah, I'll go with sterility thanks. Geez. I couldn't even conceptualize why it was a topic of conversation. If it was problematic, I wasn't going to make more vamps. I didn't want to pass along this curse to anyone else.

"How do we know that this is the same as the Immortuos in the past?" Dez ventured. "Do we have any texts on them? Can we tally their powers against

Alexandra's? Can we look at their behaviors beside hers? It's possible this is a new vampiric mutation."

"I agree, we need to look into this deeper," Magnus said. "More pressing is the general idea that we now have an animated corpse in a lower room of your home. That is our first and only order of business. Once that is dealt with, we'll consider moving on to historical studies."

Clio rose and came over to me, settled beside me, and took my hands in her own. "Can you tell us exactly what you did? Perhaps we can reverse engineer this. I remember early necromancers would de-animate corpses with the same ease they animated them. Their powers were not always used for evil, even if that's where the clan ended up."

I went over the details of my raising of Jim once more. All three of my peers asked questions and dug deeply into the details of every action and thought. At the end of it, we were none the wiser.

"Have you attempted to remove whatever magics you put upon him?" Magnus finally asked.

"No, I haven't done anything else, because I've been dealing with the fallout since it happened. I'll be honest, I've been terrified to do anything at all."

"Then let's give this a go," he stated, and rose to his feet. "Let's go look at the corpse."

"Jim," I said, my voice quiet yet insistent
"What?"

"His name is Jim," I repeated. "He's a person. And not a bad one, even if he's a dead one."

"Alexandra, it's important not to get attached to these things. You need to focus on reversing what you've done, so that he can go to his rest. Right now, his soul is trapped within his body. It's my educated opinion that it will stay trapped for all eternity if you do not reverse what you've done. Intended or not, what you have created is an abomination and it serves neither us nor him."

I nodded, and led the way down into the basement and to the safe room. I knocked first, then unlocked the door and entered. Jim was sitting on the edge of his cot, reading. He still smelled of death, but he didn't seem to have decomposed any further. I hoped my magic was holding.

"Hi Jim. This is Magnus. He is the Prince of Vancouver. He will be assisting me today."

Jim nodded acknowledgment of Magnus. "Nice to meet you." He held out his hand, still puffy and off colored. He looked at it hanging in the air between them for a moment, then lowered it. "No, I guess I wouldn't want to touch it either."

"Alexandra is going to attempt to reverse the magic she has done to you," Magnus told him bluntly. "This will result in your proper death. At that time, your soul will migrate, as it should."

"Okay, that makes sense." Jim ran a hand through his hair, and a small clump of it came out, which he dropped, his eyes wild with fear. "Will it hurt?"

"I wouldn't think so," Clio assured him. "It should be a continuation of the natural process of death".

"Wait, I had started all this to find out who murdered him," I complained. "Should we finish that first?"

"No!" I got bombarded from three sides. No, four, because even Jim had chimed in on that one.

I held up my hands in defeat. And then it hit me… no blood. I had no more of Jim's blood. How was I supposed to work magic on him without the blood? I wondered if there was still some of it on the pavement back at the murder scene.

"Jim, is there any part of you that still contains any blood?"

He thought about it for a long moment, seeming to do an inventory. "I don't think so. The last of it got washed off when I showered last night."

Clio and Magnus looked irritated. Dez looked confused. "Why does that matter?" he asked.

"Because if there's no blood, how do I reverse it? What am I going to do the magic on?" I spoke through gritted teeth, my eyes closed, enunciating each word.

"Oh. Yes, well." Dez thought about it for a bit. "Can you use another bodily fluid? Or some small bit of flesh?"

I was skeptical. "I don't think that's going to work. I mean, we work with blood. We're all about the blood."

"The Sanguinem are all about the blood, Alexandra. You, on the other hand, may not be." Magnus raised an eyebrow and gestured toward Jim. "So, let's give this a go."

"Easy for you to say," I muttered. I looked critically at Jim. I didn't see anything in the way of bodily fluids. I wasn't going to carve bits of him up. This was awful. I am not a bad person, and I did not like the idea of killing someone, even if he'd be dead now if it weren't for me.

"Think of it as being a kind of witchcraft," Clio suggested, trying to be helpful.

Ah. I was going to sniff at Clio's comment but then realized that it made sense. I helped myself to some of Jim's thinning hair, and asked Dez to fetch me some nail clippers. I snipped off a bit of Jim's nails, and then slid those and the hair into one of my blood vials. I sat down, took a deep breath, and closed my eyes. I tried to concentrate on the vial in my hands. I reached out for it, mentally. I stretched my senses, seeking out the contents. Nothing. All I could sense were all the people staring at me.

"Look, you all have to leave. I can't do this in front of an audience. Step outside, close the door, and leave me alone here with Jim for a bit. Come back in an hour if you haven't seen me." I waved them all away without opening my eyes.

I heard Magnus make a protesting sound, and what I assumed was Clio shushing him. The three of them retreated, and the door closed with its little "whoosh" of sound, and then locked. I opened my eyes and looked critically at Jim.

"You're sure you're okay with this?"

He nodded. "I don't feel like myself. I can't give you any useful information about who killed me. I don't see a reason to be here. And while I'm not feeling a whole lot, I definitely am feeling a revulsion to the idea of being trapped in a rotting, decomposing body. That sounds… considerably less than positive. So yes, I'm okay with this."

My turn to nod. "Alright. Lay down on the cot. If it works, I don't know what happens. I don't know if you'll go fast or slow. No sense things being messy."

Jim shrugged and settled onto the cot. Once he was quiet and unmoving, I closed my eyes again and tried to find my center. Much of my blood magic practice over the past year or so had been learning to find a quiet space inside my head. Once there, I could then reach out and mentally touch whatever I was working on. Meditation and reflection were things I found difficult but worthwhile. I worked at finding that place now.

I let myself become more aware of the glass vial in my hands. My fingers traced over the faint imperfections in the glass. I brought the image of it into my mind's eye, and at first that mental photograph was of a vial full of blood. I hastily corrected that. I imagined an empty vial, then worked toward 'seeing' the vial full of the hair and fingernail clippings it actually contained. I was sheened with sweat by the time I had truly captured and perfected that vision. However, it definitely connected me with the contents of the vial.

Blood had always had a particular resonance to it, as if it vibrated at a particular speed and I could feel that movement in my hands and in my brain. The contents of the vial had a different vibration, one that was much less subtle, more like a low, loud buzz. I seized on that buzz, greedily focusing all my attention on it. I pushed out with the energy I always felt rise up from the pit of my stomach, enveloping the vial in it. I felt an almost audible click at that point, and I was certain I was on the right path.

I pictured Jim on the cot, then, lifeless. I imagined his life essence leaving his body. I imagined his body returning to a normal decomposition rate. I made the vision as detailed as I could, and really focused on the idea that he was Dead dead. With an outward gush of energy, I let go.

I sat there for a long moment, unmoving, silent. Workings of that kind always left me drained. I was afraid to open my eyes, because I knew I'd been sweating, and vampires don't have regular sweat. It's a messy, bloody business, and I was glad it didn't happen often.

"I don't think it worked," Jim said from the cot.

I opened my eyes, and half slumped down. "No, apparently not." He looked no different, laying there on his back with his hands crossed over his chest. He turned his head to face me, but otherwise didn't move. I groaned, rubbing my face with my hands, frustrated. "I don't know what I'm doing."

I heard the door behind me, and Dez came back in with Clio.

"Any luck?" he asked.

"No," I grunted. I looked down at myself, noting the faint blood stains all over my clothing, and sighed. "I hate this. How the hell do I learn this stuff when there's no one to teach me? This is worse than your fucking math lessons, Dez!"

"We all learned this way at some point in the past, Alexandra," Clio said, comforting me. She crouched beside me to talk. "And not all of us had teachers, anyhow. Some of us had to figure it out as we went along. It's not impossible, even if it's rare in today's world."

"Thanks, Clio." I refused to meet her eyes, because then I'd see just how reasonable she was being. I didn't want to feel pushed into being reasonable right now. I was frustrated and upset and I wanted to stay that way.

"Does this mean I'm stuck this way?" Jim interjected. He pushed himself upright. I noticed that his skin was becoming somewhat discolored, but some of the swelling had gone down. Had my spellwork had done some of its job?

"For now, yes. I am not giving up, though." I sighed. "This is going to take a lot more investigation and research, though. Clio, do you or Magnus have any books or papers that cover anything at all about the necromancers? Something I could learn from? I don't even know what I'm supposed to be able to do, never mind how to go about doing it."

"We're not giving up," Clio corrected. "We will work together to find a solution."

Dez pulled a folding chair out from its rack and opened it, sitting in it backwards and leaning on the backrest. "We make a good team, Jim. It may take us some time, but we'll figure it out. Maybe we can get some history from you, in the meantime. Maybe there is some aspect of your murder that interfered with Alexandra's magic, for instance."

My head jerked up. "Hey, that might be worth looking into. Dez, if he was killed by something supernatural, like a vampire or a werewolf, that might mess with the magic. In theory."

Clio nodded, slow and deliberate. "Maybe. I think it's unlikely, but not impossible. Looking into it while we're waiting in limbo does seem to be a reasonable use of our time, though. Dez, Alexandra, why don't the two of you work on this aspect. I'll head back to court and see what I can dredge up in the library. We'll meet at court tomorrow, I think. Come when you can."

Unfolding from her crouch, Clio looked like a ballet dancer. Her long legs were so damn graceful, no matter what she wore. Today's flowing pant suit was no exception. I fought down a momentary surge of envy; I was beautiful in my own way, after all. It was something I was learning, slowly.

Dez pulled out a notepad from his back pocket, and a pencil from his shirt pocket. "Let's start with what happened leading up to your death, Jim."

Jim closed his eyes, concentrating on remembering. "I was walking along the trail, just enjoying the quiet. There wasn't anyone else around."

"Can you remember any sounds or smells?" I asked. Memories were funny, and scents could imprint on our brains more than sights, often. If you don't believe me, think about your favorite Thanksgiving meal, and I'll bet you are thinking of a smell, not a taste.

He paused for a long time. "There was singing. I remember a song." He covered his ears with his hands, and rocked forward and back, trying to dredge up the memory. "Not a song, but more like a humming sound? It was a voice, but not words."

Dez made quick, precise notes in his own strange shorthand. "What direction was it coming from?"

"It came from out in the water," Jim replied hesitantly. "It came in waves. Closer, then farther away. Organic."

"Okay. That's good. So you heard this sound. Did you recognize it? Had you heard it before?" I narrowed in on this fact. I didn't know why this music had stuck in Jim's muddled, murdered brain, but it had, and I was going to treat it like the clue it was.

"Yes…" He nodded, wrapping his arms around himself. "I remember hearing bits of it the last few times I went walking out there. Maybe someone was playing music on a boom box?"

"Do you want me to look into who hangs out down there at night, hon?" Dez nodded to me. "Okay, will do. You follow this line of inquiry and I'll go check it out. I'll ask a friend of mine to check into whether there have been other murders like Jim's there, too."

I slipped out, locking the door behind me. I paused in my room to change into jeans and a tee shirt, and to switch from heels to tennis shoes. I snagged my keys from the hook by the door, grabbed my purse, and went at top speed to the garage.

It was still early in the evening for me, only midnight or so. For the humans, it was late, though. Much of the activity of the day was done, and the roads were silent and empty. It was windy, but not cold, the last vestiges of spring being blown away to make room for the heat of summer. There was no moon tonight, so the dark corners of the city were blacker than usual. It didn't bother me, of course. I could see well enough in the dead of night. The Capilano Pacific Trail skirted the edge of Ambleside Beach and then curved north up the remnants of the Capilano River.

I had found Jim's body on the pavement where the beach and the river met, near the railway bridge. I started there. I held out faint hope that some remnant of blood was still lurking around for me to collect and use for my own devices. Nothing remained of the previous night's scene, however. Some industrious civil employee had cleaned the place, leaving nothing but pristine pavement and a scattering of dirt.

I looked all around the area, in the scrubby grass, and along the nearby tree line. I waded through the low river and examined the other bank as well. I found plenty of discarded condom wrappers, and a few needles. These I dutifully disposed of in the sharps containers provided by the city. There was a lot of trash, but no clues to be seen. There were no tracks to follow, no scuffle marks. Jim's first remark to me had been that it was a woman who killed him, but he wasn't a tiny guy. A woman would either have had to know him to get close enough, or she would have had to be large and bulky. Or not human, I reminded myself.

My cell phone beeped at me, and I read a message from Dez. He remembers water, and something vague about the woman's hair. Check near the water itself. I replied that I would, and again went down to the edge of the river. The tide was low, and the river was low anyhow after a year lacking in sufficient rain. There were footprints where the sandy beach met the water, but the gravel portions didn't show anything.

On a whim, I slipped out of my shoes and socks, and rolled my jeans up to my knees. I waded into the water. To me it felt normal, a little cooler than body temperature. It would be quite chilly to a human. I dug my toes into the sand, and closed my eyes. I reached out my senses and breathed in deeply.

I could smell humans nearby, and the faint hint of sex. I detected overtones of latex and chemicals, mixed in with male and female musk. Overwhelming those background odors was the distinct smell of the water itself. Seaweed and salt, fish, and that indescribable scent that is what the sea smells like. And something else.

I tried to focus on it. For a fleeting moment, it was like a fluttering of butterfly wings against my consciousness, and then it was gone. I breathed in again, but nothing remained, if anything had been there at all. I felt nothing more, to my frustration. I couldn't be sure if I had sensed something or not. I wanted to believe I had, but it was so delicate, it could have literally been anything. It might have been an errant breeze. I growled to myself, and waded back to shore.

I spent the next three hours combing the area. I walked through the empty golf course, and sprinted along the pitch black pathway from the beach to the nearby mall. I even jogged along a couple of miles of the railroad track, hoping to find something. Vampiric powers are awesome, in that I didn't get cold or tired, and didn't need a flashlight. I avoided the handful of humans wandering around, except for the young man who decided he was going to try and mug me. He got special treatment. When I was done with him, I left him with a soul crushing sense of disappointment in his personal life choices.

By 4:00 a.m., I had combed the area as thoroughly as I could. There was nothing that stood out, nothing I could consider as evidence. What little evidence I had known about was gone. I gave up and returned to my car, buckled in, and headed home. I tried not to allow my anger at the situation to overcome me.

On the way back, I paused in at our local police station. I had made friends with the older clerk that worked nights at the front desk. She was a pleasant sort, rather short and round of face, but pretty and bubbly. Dez and I had come to know her when we were making the local cops aware of some of our parties. We attempted to be good citizens of the area, after all, and didn't want officers visiting us about noise complaints.

I had worked hard at making the local constabulary believe that I was an unsuccessful writer of articles. It gave me an excuse to ask for information without sounding too much like a busy-body. The fact that I hadn't gotten anything published (because I hadn't actually written anything) wasn't unusual. The west coast always attracted a lot of odd people doing odd things. I was "odd like everyone else."

As I walked into the station, Sgt. Bouchard looked up from her computer. "Oh hey!" she said, smiling. "I haven't seen you in ages. How are you and Dez doing?"

"Oh, we're fine. It's been a quiet winter, and we stayed indoors for the most part. I like fires and not shoveling snow." We both chuckled.

"What can I do for you tonight?" She rose from her seat and came to the counter, leaning forward in a friendly way. She smelled relaxed, and I guessed the night had been a quiet one.

"Well, I am working on writing up a history of murders in the area. Someone told me you found a guy a few weeks back, dead on a pathway down near the Capilano River. I couldn't find a news report. Do you know anything about that?" I pulled out my 'author's notebook' and a pencil from my purse. It was a long shot, referencing a murder that I wasn't sure had happened or been reported. If similar crime scenes had been investigated, it would be helpful to know, though.

"Oh, you do write about juicy stuff, don't you?" she said. "I haven't heard anything, but let me go check, okay?" She trundled off to the back filing cabinet and thumbed through the piles of reports there. Two she set to the side, and the rest were returned to their precarious tower.

"So these are public, and were reported to the local newspapers, but nothing came up. I'm not sure which one your friend was referring to, but if it's a general story, either might do you. This one," she slid a folder over the Formica counter top, "was found on the beach near the wastewater plant, down under the Lion's Gate Bridge."

I pulled the file folder closer and flipped it open. There were a couple of photographs of evidence cones, and an artist's sketch of the victim, as well as what information they had on him. It was pretty devoid of details, to be expected since it was a public news release.

"Can I take a couple of pics of this for my files?" I asked.

The sergeant nodded, and pushed the second file to me. I used my phone to take pictures of each page in the first file. I opened the second file and noted the location was fairly close to the first one. It was also near Jim's spot, south of a paintball place, in a treed area. I snapped photos of that file, too.

I was in the process of sending all the information to Dez and Clio, when my phone binged at me. An image, from Dez, of Jim's driver's license. I cropped the image, and showed it to the sergeant. "One last question. Have you ever had a run-in with this guy?"

She looked at the image, and shook her head. "I don't remember him. Of course, he might not have ever been in this station. Why are you looking for him?"

I shrugged. "I got the picture from someone who said he was hanging around down near the beach in the area. Nothing solid, though. If it turns out to be a real tip, I'll send it your way for sure."

"Sounds good. You have a good night, now!

4 – More on Death

When I got home, I went straight to my own room on the upper floor of the house. My computer was set up there, and I wanted to get all the pictures loaded onto the hard drive. That done, I wandered downstairs again. Dez was sitting in one of the big, comfy chairs I'd purchased for the family room, staring out the double doors into the backyard. He looked up as I came in, and smiled.

"Come sit, love, and tell me about what you've found." He shifted to the couch and patted the spot beside him.

I flopped down beside him and nestled myself against his side. I told him everything I'd found at the scene of the crime, meaning nothing at all. I pulled up a map of the area on my phone and showed him the locations where the other bodies had been found. It was pretty obvious they were connected. They were all within two miles of each other. The crime scenes all looked pretty similar, per the files I'd copied. The bodies were found close to the water, but definitely on dry land, and had multiple gut wounds that led to bleeding out. Autopsy reports hadn't come in yet, but everything seemed to point to the blood loss as the cause of death.

"It all appears to line up with what happened to Jim. Right down to the type of gut wounds." I sighed, rubbed my temples, and tried to relax.

"I agree. The question is, do the local police have a serial killer on their hands, and we ignore it? Or do we have a supernatural problem on our hands, and we deal with it?" Dez looked over the artist renderings of the victims once more. "I'm not seeing a lot of similarities between the men. They don't look alike. They aren't dressed alike. They don't appear to be from the same economic levels, either. This one had keys to a Lexus in his pocket, and this one didn't even have $10.00 in his ratty wallet."

"Frankly, if it's just a serial killer, I might take care of her myself. I'm irritated enough that she'd probably taste good," I grumped.

Dez chuckled. "Our mighty prince might even give permission for that kind of hunt," he agreed. "Perhaps a bounty for the vampire that takes her down." The amusement seeped out of his voice as he continued, though. "On the other hand, we might be on the hunt regardless. If this is human, dealing with it will be easy. If it's supernatural, it will be a lot more difficult. I'm not even sure what it would be. Not vampire; we don't hunt this way."

"It wasn't anything, Dez. There wasn't any scent there. All I could smell was humans. I mean, I didn't even catch a whiff of another vampire. Just humans, and water, really."

"Well, you did good with your police friend at least. Now we know someone or something is operating locally. We can also see if Jim knows either of these two." Dez indicated the sketches on my phone.

"Yeah. Hey, did he remember anything more?" I shifted, turning so I could sit cross legged on the couch and face Dez. "Did you guys talk for long?"

"I questioned him for a couple of hours. His memory is full of holes. I don't think he's faking any of it, either. I suspect it's the lack of oxygen to the brain matter. He's trying, though. He did mention the woman's hair was green, but couldn't remember if it was a more natural hue or if it was the vibrant green the kids use these days."

"Who does security stuff? Magnus will know." I pulled up the map again, giving a critical look at the area. "There should be cameras around. Can we access them? The bridge has cameras on it, and the outside of the water treatment plant might as well. If we're looking for a female with green hair, regardless of shade, she ought to stand out on video."

"Good idea. Let Clio know to pass that one along to the prince. I'm going to go eat, and I'll meet you in the bedroom in an hour or so." He pushed up from the couch with a grunt.

I called Clio right away. "Hey you. I thought of something. The water processing plant is where another body was found, and it should have cameras, right?" I filled in all the various details for her.

"That's good, Alexandra. I'll have one of our people look into that. Green hair seems odd, doesn't it?"

"Nah. Lots of people dye their hair odd colors these days, Clio. It's pretty normal. Though vibrant green is not as popular a color, so I'm hoping it'll give us a lead."

"That would be nice," she agreed.

"I also have some thoughts. If I'm supposed to be some kind of necromancer, then I should have some other powers over the dead, right?"

There was a distinct pause before Clio responded. "Yes. Though you should be careful about how you play with that."

"I'm not going to raise any other dead things, hon. I figured if I can't de-animate Jim, I could work at halting the decomposition process. Dez worries that he's forgetting things because his brain isn't functioning well due to lack of oxygen. I thought I could attempt to work some magic that will arrest the symptoms of death."

"Symptoms of death. That sounds very wrong, Alexandra." Clio giggled, though she sounded more sedate than usual. "Be careful, hon. Necromancy is difficult to master. It went wrong for so many people."

"Yeah, I have a lot of questions about that. But not now; I have too much to do. I promise to be careful, though."

I privately promised myself I would be careful. I didn't want to 'go evil' on people, and I didn't want to make any accidental mistakes, either. I needed to think this out before I did anything.

I let myself into the safe room, and found Jim sitting on the cot. He wasn't doing anything at all. He sat there, kind of staring at the wall.

"Jim?"

He looked over at me, his movements slow, then seemed to wake up somewhat. "Hi. I remember you."

"Yeah, I'm Alexandra," I offered. Maybe he was just bad at names. Maybe his brain was rotting inside his skull. Didn't matter much which was true, to be honest. "I hear you and Dez talked for a long time. That's good. I am hoping you'll talk with me for a while, too."

"Sure."

Jim continued to sit there and stare at me, or possibly through me. I sighed, a strangled sound, knowing this was my fault and not his. He couldn't help being out of it.

"I want to get some information about you, and then I'm hoping to try another working to see if I can help a bit."

"Okay."

"Can you tell me what you did before? Where did you work? What was your life like? What's your last name?"

"I'm Jim. James. James Hale."

More silence. I realized I would need to ask one question at a time. He couldn't handle more than that. "How old are you?"

"I'm 39. I was born in November. November 12, 1979."

Okay, we were making progress, albeit slow progress. "And what did you do for a living?"

"I'm a financial risk analyst. I look for risks that could damage clients' assets, and I do a lot of statistical analysis. It's not very exciting from the outside, but I've always been good at it."

"Who did you work for?"

"It's a holding company. The official name is Private Holdings Inc, but it's a numbered business."

"Okay, so not a well known company, likely. Did you do any accounts that were dangerous? Criminal accounts or gangs?"

"I… I don't think so?" His words came out more as a question than a statement.

"Are you sure? You don't sound sure."

"I did risk assessment on accounts for banks and big corporations. That wasn't dangerous."

I gave him a moment, then prompted, "But something was dangerous?"

"No." He shook his head. "No, work was fine."

I tilted my head, thinking. "Was something else dangerous?"

"No."

The stilted conversation was giving me a headache. I decided to take the conversation elsewhere and see if that was better. "Are you married?" I asked.

"No, I am not."

"Kids?"

"I… no."

I watched his face. During most of the conversation, his muscles had been quite slack, reminiscent of the zombies from television. Asking about marriage and kids, though, had caused him to flinch. His voice had hardened, as well. It was almost imperceptible, but perhaps I was onto something.

"Thinking about kids?" I pressed.

He shifted on the cot, and stared at the wall behind me. "Maybe. I don't really remember."

There. That was the first time I'd heard him lie. Before, when he was talking about not remembering, it was obvious that he was searching for memories. This time, it was an avoidance mechanism. I'm not sure what it was about kids, but he remembered something. I wondered what.

"No problem. This must be very stressful for you. I'm going to be trying some sustaining workings, to help you hold onto yourself, physically. I'm hoping it will halt any deterioration of your body and such."

"Okay."

"It's going to take me a bit to figure this out. Just relax. You don't need to do anything anyhow."

He nodded, and returned to the blank stare and slightly open mouth that he'd been wearing when I entered. I watched him out of the corner of my eye as I made some notes in my book. All movement ceased. His eyes seemed to almost glaze over. It was disconcerting.

Blood magic, of the type Dez practiced, had always eluded me. I was beginning to understand why. If I wasn't a blood mage, then I would not have gained the affinity for blood magic that comes with being a member of the Sanguinem bloodline. I had some of the abilities, because necromancy was an offshoot of blood magic, but not all of them. It meant there was a host of abilities that I might have, that I had yet to discover.

Blood magic used the blood of a person to influence them, or others' view of them. Necromancy influenced dead people. How about dead animals? Could I animate those? Maybe the right thing to do was to animate something small, and then experiment with it. If nothing else, it might give me some hints as to why I couldn't send Jim back to whatever abyss I'd dragged him from. Necromancy might work better on whole bodies, or on parts of bodies. Heads, for instance, might be the equivalent of blood to necromancy. My own head reeled as I contemplated the possibilities.

Alright, if I was going to do blood magic, I would take a vial of blood and 'reach out' to it, sensing it with my own energy. That's what I was doing when I accidentally animated Jim. So blood was something I could use. I could be a hybrid blood mage and necromancer combined. That, or blood might just be useful to a necromancer. I groaned to myself.

Location stones were easy for me now. If I smeared charged blood onto a stone, I could use it to locate the blood's owner, or their vampire family. Like calls to like, if you wanted to talk like a witch.

How could I apply that idea to maintaining Jim's body and brain?

Wait. What if I used vital blood, human blood, from a donor. I could make Jim himself 'the stone', and smear it on him, and infuse him with the energy contained within the blood. That might work!

"Be right back." Jim didn't move as I bounced up and sprinted for the door. It's possible he didn't see me move. I was going at vamp speed, which was quicker than most humans tracked. Jim seemed to be a tad slower at the moment than even slow humans. Regardless, I was out the door, up to the kitchen to fetch a blood bag, and back down and in the room within a minute.

I yanked a vial out of my purse and dribbled some of the blood into it. In the process, I managed to drip it on myself, and I licked my fingers and my wrist to clean them. I wasn't paying attention to that, though. I set the bag aside and cradled the vial between my hands. Eyes closed, I reached out mentally to the blood. I willed it to be warm and vital and energetic, as it had been within its owner's body. I infused the blood with a sense of life, focusing on the preservation of the host body. When I felt the magical click of it locking into place, I opened my eyes. The vial glowed and pulsed, and I grinned.

"Jim?" He looked up, slowly. "I'm going to put some of this on your forehead, and then you're going to drink the rest of it."

"I'm not thirsty," he said, his voice thick as if he'd awoken from a heavy sleep.

"Doesn't matter," I stated. "This isn't for quenching thirst, this is magic." I got some of the blood onto my index finger, and drew a thick red cross on his forehead. "Invigorate," I said under my breathe, not the English word, but the Latin, sounding more like en-veeg-or-ah-tay. I handed Jim the vial.

He took it, hesitant, and upended the contents into his mouth. As he swallowed, I could see the faint glow of the blood actually spread to touch much of his upper body. Yes!

"How do you feel?" I demanded.

"Better," he admitted, and when he caught my eye, there was less glaze and more intelligence there. His self-awareness had come back, at least somewhat.

"Good. I have no idea how long that will work. However, let's take it for what it is. For right now, it's a success."

There was a knock at the door then, and Dez entered. His eyes narrowed; I could tell he immediately sensed the difference in Jim.

"I tried something else. Rather than trying to reverse the previous magic, I went for a sustaining spell instead. I'm hoping it'll halt the degeneration and give us some more time." I smiled to him, triumph making me feel a tad giddy.

"Excellent. That's good work. For all that we've gotten nowhere this evening, our short summer night is done. It's time for bed, my love. Will you be alright here Jim? Is there anything you need?"

"No, I think I'm good. I have a pencil and paper. If this fades, I'll try and remember to note down when, okay?"

"That's helpful," I smiled. "Thank you. This was a good step forward."

Dez and I exited, locking the poor man into our safe room once more. He headed for the bedroom, but I wasn't having any of that. I'd grubbed around in dirty areas for hours, and he'd been heavens knew where getting something to eat. I snatched his wrist and yanked him toward the large and sumptuous bathroom we shared.

⊱⊰

As we lay in bed and awaited the undeniable sleep of the day together, we talked over the various aspects of our day. I cuddled up against Dez's side, happy to finally be in my favorite place.

"So what do I call myself now?" I asked. The knowledge that I wasn't a blood mage had been bouncing around in my skull since I had been told. It made perfect sense, when you added up all the variables. I was horrid at the blood magic the rest of the Sanguinem performed. There were other aspects, though, that I could do which were far beyond them. I wondered what else I could do.

"I suppose it'll be up to you, for the most part. If you are the founder of a new bloodline, a new family, then the choice will be yours. We tend to go with Latin names. The necromancers were called Immortuos before. It's the Latin word for 'undead', because they took corpses and animated them. Alex, hon, we don't know if you are one of them anyhow. You could be something different, something new."

I tilted my head and looked up at him. "Really, now. Come on, Dez, Clio was looking at me like I had three heads. Magnus couldn't meet my eye. Right now, he's trying to decide whether he's only going to pull out my teeth, or whether he's going to have to kill me."

He looked as if he were going to argue, and then stopped himself. "You're right. They both have memories of that time. I do not. They know what it was like. The topic has come up before, at court and within our own ranks. Necromancy is a branch of blood magic, make no mistake. You cannot have one without the other. You are my progeny, and this problem came about because of me. Your life is not the only one on the line."

I buried my face in his chest. "I'm sorry. I feel like this is all my fault!"

"It is not, Alexandra. We don't choose these things. It's akin to evolution, I suppose. And let's be honest. I was told that necromancers were around for hundreds of years before they became a problem. The issue may have nothing at all to do with the magic. It could be that the 16th century was a time of rampant superstition mixed with stupid people doing stupid things. Remember, they didn't know anymore back then than what was in front of them. We can look back now, and decide that it was a transient problem. They didn't have the big picture we now have."

"So you're saying that some of the necromancers could have been innocent and were killed for kicks?" I frowned, and he tightened his arms around me.

"Yes, unfortunately. Vampires, like humans, sometimes get caught up in mobs. It isn't pretty, no matter who's doing it. The bottom line is, you are not directly connected with those in the past who did terrible things in the name of our people. Whether you share their powers and skills, you do not share their blood. You share mine." He squeezed me. "We deal with this as we always do: day by day. And speaking of days, tell me about this new idea for your walking corpse."

We both sat up to face one another. I folded my legs into a half lotus position, and pushed my hair out of my eyes. "We were thinking that as a necromancer it wasn't as much about blood. But you pointed out that I come from you and the Sanguinem. That means it has to have something to do with blood. I still have no idea how to undo what I've done, but I thought if blood sustains us, then it might also sustain Jim. And it sure did something."

Dez nodded. "I agree. He was much more normal looking when I came in."

"I think that human blood can help him to maintain his current health level. I need to read about the necromancers of the past, Dez, so I can learn about what they did. I'm okay with reverse engineering magic, but I have no idea what I might be able to do or not do. I'm hoping Clio and Magnus will have some books for me to read, or some information to go over. I need ideas."

"Well, the idea you've had so far seems to be a good one. Your magic has always been much more organic. That's fine."

"I was thinking I should experiment on small things. Rodents, for instance."

"Animating them?" Dez's eyes narrowed. "Do we want undead rats running around the place, rotting? Because that's how you get undead rats."

"I would keep them in a cage, Dez. The idea would be to see what I could do to them that might remove their animation. If I can de-animate a rat corpse, then I should be able to transfer the idea from rat to Jim. I don't want to experiment on Jim himself, though. What if I made it worse?"

"I'm not sure how to make it worse for him than it currently is, but I do see your point. We need to seek Magnus out and ask him to share his wisdom on the subject, though. Until then, no messing around with new magic, please. If your invigoration spell holds well enough with Jim, we can all go to court tomorrow evening. He looked pretty normal earlier."

"Sounds good. By the by, did he say anything to you about kids or a wife?"

Dez thought for a moment. "No, we didn't touch on the subject. Why?"

"I asked him earlier if he was married or had kids, and I swear he flinched. I mean, I guess it could be me, but I am convinced he was being shifty about something. I can't figure out why, though."

"He was dressed when you found him, right? Did he have a wedding band?"

I looked over the image in my mind's eye. "I didn't see one. His finger isn't indented or funny colored, though, so no indications of a wedding ring anytime lately."

"I wondered if he was cheating on his wife, and that's why he was out walking in the dead of night. It would explain why he didn't want to talk about marriage or kids."

"I guess so. Though we don't know exactly what time he was walking around. I happened to have found his body in the wee hours. I admit, it would have been odd for it not to be discovered by someone other than me, had he been there a while. Maybe it was a body dump?"

Dez shook his head. "No, his body isn't degraded enough to have been dead much longer than an hour or so before you found him."

"Right. How do we know that?"

"Bodies have a very standard pattern for decomposing, hon. Your magic halted or slowed the process, but it's obvious he hasn't been dead for more than a couple of hours. We can assume relatively safely that most of the decomp we're seeing in him happened prior to your finding him."'

"That makes sense. This is all so bloody confusing, though. Why is he still decomposing, anyhow? If I'm a necromancer, doesn't that mean I get to raise people and they look normal?"

"There are levels, Alexandra. You created the magic that sustains his soul. Your magic affected his soul, his essence. It didn't do much of anything but a staying action for his body. His body is going to continue to do what it does. It doesn't contain the kind of magic that sustains our bodies along with our minds. There's a lot more to creating a vampire. I doubt it's possible to do that by accident."

"How are vampires made?" I tugged at the sheets laying over my body. "I have no idea how you made me. It never occurred to me to ask. But I should know, shouldn't I?"

"I'm not sure I want to tell you right now, Alex." Dez's voice was soft but serious, the deep tone rich with unspoken emotion. "There is enough going on right now that I suspect it would not be good to pass along at this point. Right now I can tell Magnus and everyone else that you don't know how to make progeny. Since you didn't know how, it was never a motive in your raising of this zombie."

I stared at him, eyes dark and hooded. "Did you just suggest that I was trying to make a vampire behind your back?"

He closed his eyes and counted to ten. "No, love, I did not. But it's something that might come to other people, if they put their minds to it."

"I see." I pursed my lips, fighting the anger. "I guess that I haven't proven myself to be reliable yet."

"It's not that, Alexandra. You're only two years old! We don't know you well. In the eyes of someone like Magnus, or Clio, that's a nanosecond of life. Clio has shoes older than ME, never mind you."

"I hear you. It's just… I've tried so hard to be good and right, and to be helpful wherever possible. I follow the rules. I do things for the community. And now, all because of something I apparently have no control over whatsoever, I'm going to be judged. And I'm not going to be judged on what I do or don't do. I'm going to be judged based on what some people did 400 years ago! It's not fair, and it's not right!"

"You are correct. It's not fair. But we are going to show them that just because you're a necromancer does not mean you're like the ones that died. You helped a lot with the workings from Egypt last year. That may have been because your magic called to it. You may be able to do more toward extending the lives of your fellow vampires than all my research and attempts. You may be the key."

"I hope you're right."

For the first time in a long time, I thanked whatever holy things existed for our kind, for the mercy of the undeniable sleep that dawn brought. Usually it irritated me, but if I had been left to my own devices, I'd never have gotten to sleep that night. Dawn forced the issue, and I let it take me unfought.

5 – Jim's Story

When I awoke, Dez was already gone. A note written in his impeccable handwriting lay on the pillow beside me. Showering, then going to my office. Come find me. D. I pulled on a pair of jeans and a "Hail Bacon" t shirt, and padded to the bathroom. I brushed my teeth, staring at the image reflected in the mirror. I found myself wondering about the myth of vampires having no reflection. Perhaps it had something to do with the silver backing on old mirrors. Today's ones were made of mirrored paper plastered onto glass, after all. No silver involved.

Then there was the whole teeth brushing thing. Did I even need to do it now? My teeth didn't seem to decay at all. Despite squalid living conditions for some of the vampires, I'd never seen one with bad teeth. They all looked perfect. In fact, now that I was actually thinking about it, I hadn't ever seen a vampire with so much as a single missing tooth. Did the magic that animated us also regenerate our teeth? I didn't know, and I wasn't worried. Regardless, my mouth always tasted like a bag full of cotton in the morning. Teeth brushing was going to continue to be a thing, whether it was essential or not.

I stared at myself in the mirror, examining all the details of my upper body. I had let my hair grow a little longer, out of the short crop and into a shoulder length sweep that flattered my face. I wasn't sure how my hair could continue growing despite my being dead. Still, I appreciated the outcome. It came almost to my shoulders, but I could pull it into a ponytail now. If I felt adventurous, I could even pin it up in different styles.

Today, I pulled the sides into a clip, and pinned it out of the way at the top of my head. I thought about makeup but decided against it. I had faced facts long before becoming a vampire; I was never going to be one of those made up girly girls.

I found Dez ensconced at his desk, poring through something on his computer. He didn't look up, but beckoned to me and waved, without looking, at a nearby chair. At least I assumed it was the chair, because otherwise I had no idea what the hand waving was about.

"What's up, babe?" I peeked over his arm, and saw that he was reading something from Magnus' court archives. "Everything okay?"

"Things are fine. I've been looking into the history of necromancy. It looks like some of the oldest vampires we know of may have been necromancers. What I'm trying to figure out is whether they were necromancers before or after they were turned. Humans practiced necromancy back then, too. All sorts of magic, in fact. Well, still do in some places. Anyhow…"

Humans practicing magic. That was not a new concept, but the idea of them doing it today was definitely a thought that hadn't occurred to me. I knew the ancient Egyptians had practiced magic, but my mind had difficulty wrapping around the modern application. On the other hand, if there was anyone practicing necromancy, I could ply them for knowledge.

"So is the human version of necromancy anything like the vampiric version? Can I learn from them?"

Dez shook his head no. "Humans and vampires don't use the same energies at all. And what humans do with necromancy is definitely not something you want to copy anyhow." He frowned

"Okay, but did you find out anything useful?"

Over the next hour, Dez explained what he knew about vampiric necromancers. Per the lore, there were a lot of necromancers in ancient Egypt and Mesopotamia, and they did a lot of good things.

The pyramids, it seems, were built by undead servitors created by necromancers. They weren't slaves by our definition, because they offered themselves up to secure freedom for loved ones. Servitors got a lot of work done, because they didn't need sleep. Also, they could work during the day as well as in the dark. This made them excellent guardians of vampires.

It was true that necromancers could use their powers to punish or torture people, but it didn't start out that way. Dez pointed out that any vampire, historical or modern, could do horrible things in a variety of messy ways. It was the people and not the clan that were problematic. He showed me some of the scanned documents from the late 1500s. A variety of people were threatened with continual undeath by the local necromancers. The vampire community there had dealt with it by banishing the few who'd misused their powers.

Necromancers could raise the dead, as I knew. They could maintain the body of their servitors, as well. The longer servitors were animated, the quicker they degenerated. There were certain spells that maintained their animation. The documents didn't explain the spells, unfortunately.

Servitors didn't feel pain or discomfort, and weren't affected by cold and heat of the weather variety. They could be damaged by severe cold and fire. Destruction of the body did not release the soul. The soul would continue to cling, conscious, to whatever part of the body remained. Lacking a body with which to communicate, they slowly went insane if not released. Some necromancers had specialized in finding trapped souls and releasing them, whatever that meant.

We could also do something that was akin to half raising the dead. We could awaken the consciousness of the dead person to ask questions of them, and then allow them to lapse into full death. This could only happen when the body was quite fresh, though. Very experienced necromancers could even raise those long dead, but their bodies would not be restored in any way. They would be animated corpses, in whatever state they awoke. It was horrifying.

During the last few years the necromancers existed, they seemed to go insane, as a group. They would snatch humans and demand service from them. If the human refused, they would kill them, animate them, put them into a magical sleep. Their bodies would then be turned over to the local constabulary. The police would declare them dead, and then they would be buried. Unfortunately for the victim, they would awaken hours later, in the dark, in a box. There they would stay, as their body rotted and their soul remained rooted to their last resting place. According to one author, there might be thousands of these trapped, insane souls around Europe.

By the time we got through that part, I was pretty much done.

"That's awful!" I hugged myself, unable to find words sufficient to my displeasure.

"It was," Dez agreed. "I think you can understand why they were destroyed."

"Were they all like that, though? You have to wonder. If they were, does that mean I'll become like that? Because I'd rather die first." I was vehement on that point. I would not want to be that person. I'd destroy myself first.

"It could be that there were decent ones around, who felt they couldn't fight against their fellow family members. I don't think the destruction mobs were all that concerned about small details. Pogroms rarely are." Dez put an arm around me. "This is not like the madness of the Impotentes, hon. I promise. You are not going to become a vicious torturer because of this. You are you, and that's not going to change."

I made assenting sounds, but I wasn't convinced. I knew he meant it, but he didn't know anything for certain. He was making comforting noises for my benefit. I appreciated that, but I could not accept them at face value.

"Let's go talk to Jim. Maybe things have changed. Or not changed." I left the office and headed for the safe room. Dez closed his laptop and followed, quiet and introspective.

Jim was awake, and still alert. He looked up when we came in, and offered greeting. I considered that a small win; his body didn't seem to be decaying any further. The scent of putrefaction had dissipated, too. His eyes, though, had a dark and glassy look to them.

"It's good to see you looking a bit more yourself," I said.

"I feel better. I didn't sleep, but I did think about things a lot."

"That sounds positive," I encouraged him. "What were you thinking about?"

"I was thinking about the woman. The one who killed me."

I perked up, and Dez appeared to be paying more attention, too. "What did you remember?"

"She was naked. I think I told you that earlier. But she was wet. Her hair was wet."

"Okay, wet is different. Was it like she just got out of the water, maybe?" The river was right there where I'd found his body, and it ran a few hundred feet into the ocean. That could make sense. Was she hiding in the water?

"She came from the water," he stated, sure of himself.

"Did you watch her come out of the water?" Dez asked in his no-nonsense tone.

Jim turned to Dez and nodded. "I saw her. There was a ripple. I was walking near the train bridge. Then I saw the ripple. I looked, and there she was. She stood up, and she was bare. Long hair, she had, and it had stuff in it."

"Stuff?" I frowned, thinking. "Like seaweed?"

"Yes, stringy stuff. Her eyes were black, so black." Jim began to shiver, and his eyes slid shut. "The overhead path light was out, so it was dark, but she looked kind of green. And her hair, it was like it was made of the same stringy stuff, even though it wasn't. But it looked that way."

"So she came up out of the water, and onto the beach area?" I tried to hold a mental image of the place where we'd been. The water wasn't all that deep right there, and I wondered if they'd been closer to the beach area and then moved toward the bridge.

"No, it was at the river. The beach was farther down. I had walked under the bridge toward

Ambleside. And that's where she came from. From the depths of the water near the dog area. She swam over, stood up out of it, and came to me. And the gravel didn't crunch under her feet, though it made plenty of sound under mine."

I looked at Dez over Jim's head. He returned my gaze, and shrugged.

"So she walked over to you. And then what?"

Jim's hand went to his chest again, a slight tremor to it. "Her nails were like knives, they were long and sharp. They grew, and then she pushed them through me. Then there was pain, lots of pain, and blood." His voice trailed off to nothing, and he gripped his chest with one hand, and the edge of his cot with the other.

"She killed you with her nails?" My suspension of disbelief was being tried. Jim had been stabbed, not clawed at.

"Yes. Her face wasn't human. It wasn't human at all." His voice, which had been flat and unemotional during most of the conversation, wavered.

"What was it then?" My forehead wrinkled in concentration as I tried to understand the myriad of details he was providing.

"Her body looked like it was human. Rail thin, but real, you know? But her face, it looked as if it had been stretched long. Her nose, it didn't poke out. It was more like two slits, almost. And her eyes were too big."

I listened to this, and thoughts rumbled around in my head. I wasn't going to say anything in front of

Jim about this, but I had no idea what our girl might be. What I knew she wasn't, was human.

"It's alright. You don't have to think about it anymore right now." I patted Jim's shoulder in a friendly way. "Is there anything you need? I believe Dez and I need to go out tonight, but we will make sure you're taken care of. More blood perhaps?"

"No, not right now. But I want to go with you. I don't want to be alone. I'm… afraid." He hung his head, shame on his puffy face.

"I know you want to come with us, but we can't do that, Jim. It would be bad. Listen, do you have any kin that you need to inform of your death? Anyone who would notice you missing?" Dez asked.

"No. No one really knew me. Work maybe, though who knows, maybe they won't notice either."

I felt rather sorry for Jim, to be honest. He had no one to miss him, no one to care if he lived or died. Maybe the woman had done him a service, in some strange way.

"Well, we'll make sure there are some books for you," Dez offered. "I'll see that you're brought several. Some playing cards, perhaps?"

Jim nodded, morose and dejected. I gathered he'd been hoping to leave the room, but he didn't fight the decision. My heart hurt for him. I couldn't imagine being cooped up like that. I had a hard enough time dealing with the fact that I couldn't go out during the day, and I wasn't even awake then!

❦

Dez and I headed out to court in his car. I settled into the heated leather seat with a soft sigh of decadent happiness. Mortal or immortal, it didn't matter: heated leather seats always felt awesome.

As we pulled out of our driveway and onto the road, I turned to face him. "Do you think that he was killed by another kind of supernatural being?"

"It's likely," Dez agreed. "I don't know too many human women who have elongated faces, black eyes, and green skin." His voice dripped with sarcasm.

"Mermaid?" I suggested, grasping at straws.

"What?" Dez looked away from the road for a long moment, staring at me. "Are you joking? There's no such thing as mermaids. Silly girl." He reached over and tugged at my hair with a fond smile.

I pouted. "I'm not silly. You told me that folk myths tend to be based on real things. So mermaids are out in the ocean, right, and lure sailors to their deaths on the rocks. What if that's the legend, but there are things behind the legend, and that's what killed Jim?"

Dez stared at the road for several miles, mulling that one over. "I'm going to defer that one to our lord and master at court," he finally responded. "It's above my pay grade. I think it's unlikely. As Sherlock Holmes was wont to say, though, once you've ruled out the impossible, whatever is left is the truth."

We went straight to court, not pausing to eat. There was always something (or someone) you could nibble on at court these days. Since Vampire

Christmas, Magnus had been keeping something around so people didn't get hangry. We arrived at the BC Fisheries building at about 11:00pm, and rode the elevator up in silence.

Clio was waiting in the hallway. "He's expecting you, though you're earlier than he thought you'd be," she commented. She hugged me, nodded to Dez. "I'm afraid he's busy right now. It'll be a while.

"It's fine, Clio. Perhaps you can go over some things with us."

Clio led us into one of the many offices lining the hallways that led to the Prince's courtroom. This one contained a large, rectangular meeting table surrounded by several chairs. A pot of coffee was perking at one end. I eyed this obscenity and then stared at Clio with burning hatred.

"You are just too much, you know," I muttered. "How dare you."

"What?" She looked confused, then followed my gaze and made a quiet, "Oh…"

"Yeah. Why would you do that? Brew coffee you know damn well I still crave and can no longer drink? Why? Bitch." I plopped my ass into one of the fake leather chairs. I gritted my teeth at the squeaking sound it emitted as it tilted back a bit.

"I'm so sorry, Alexandra. I forget that it's something you like. I was brewing it because Magnus is in the court with some people from other cities. They brought their servants with them, and I thought they'd appreciate it." She pursed her lips and sighed to herself.

"It's fine, I'll live. Sort of," I grumbled. Dez chuckled to himself, though he tried to hide it behind a cough. I made dagger eyes at him, and held my breath.

"What have you found out?" Dez settled himself into another chair, pushing it back into a semi-reclining position. "Did you manage to get into the library stacks and find anything?"

"Yes and no," Clio answered. "I did some work in there, and found a variety of things. But I also dredged through my own memories. I have been around a bit longer than most of you. I remember a time when the Immortuos were considered a powerful force for good in the world. I also remember when they were exterminated." She stopped, her long fingers tracing the pattern of the wood grain.

"I did some research of my own," I ventured. "I learned a few things. I also did something with Jim that seemed to have worked at slowing down his decomposition."

"Oh? Good for you, Alexandra!" Clio smiled.

I explained how I'd invigorated Jim's system with an infusion of blood, similar to how we use blood.

"That makes sense to me," she nodded. "It matches my memories, too. I remember the old Volvas, the witches in Scandinavia, using blood to heal wounds in bodies that were dead. It was part of preparing the body for its trip to Valhalla or Hel, to the afterlife. Sometimes, months after a warrior's death, he would be sighted again. At the time, we assumed they were doing Odin's work, though now I realize they must have been vampires. Many of our witches and healers were vampires, or other supernatural creatures. It wasn't until much later, though, that the Immortuos began torturing humans. And other vampires."

"Yeah, but it started out good, Clio. The pyramids and mummies, all that stuff. It wasn't all bad." I grimaced. "I'm not the people who went bad. Besides, it's possible they didn't all go bad. And let's be honest, it's also possible there are other necromancers out there who are hidden. You know, because they're terrified you're going to burn them to dust if they're found." I pursed my lips.

"It's a valid concern," Clio admitted, her voice sad. "Prejudice runs deep, and memories are long in the vampire community. Even those who weren't there have heard the stories from their Elders."

I shot a pissy look at Dez. "Well, some of us have. Others haven't. Apparently some elders don't pass on those stories."

Clio looked from me to Dez and back. "Something I need to know about?" she asked.

"Nope," I said shortly. I stared angrily at the coffee maker, which had finished brewing. It was now emitting that wonderful smell that always lied to me about how good it would taste.

"She's upset with me," Dez explained after a short pause. "I didn't tell her not to play with dead things and she's irritated with me."

Clio's left eyebrow shot up about three inches. "You… what?"

"I didn't mean to raise Jim. I wanted to find out who killed him. We've done that, sort of, by the way. Regardless, Dez thinks I should 'just know' that it's wrong to use dead blood in rituals, but I disagree. As I've pointed out several times, we ourselves are dead. What makes Jim's type of dead less worthy of experimentation? I mean, I'm sorry I've done something that's currently irreversible, but other than that, I don't consider it wrong."

"I couldn't say," Clio murmured.

A faint knock at the door interrupted our conversation. A human peeked into the conference room, and noted the three somber vampires clustered at one end.

"We were looking for the coffee," the tall, blonde haired male ventured. "One of the guards said to look in here."

I beckoned for them to enter. "It's here. Come get some. Then turn it off, for the sake of all that's holy, and leave please."

A group of three humans entered, and scurried to the coffee machine. The delectable smell wafted about, and I groaned. One of the two females eyed me, nervous.

"She's fine," Dez assured her. "Alexandra here drank a lot of coffee as a human, and was recently welcomed into our ranks. She still craves her caffeine despite death. You can relax, though. She knows it doesn't taste very good when filtered through blood." He snickered to himself, and I made grumpy noises. Clio smiled fondly at us both.

The humans remained somewhat wary, but not afraid. They came and emptied the coffee pot, then did the kindness of rinsing it before returning it. I mouthed my thanks to the original male who'd come in. He grinned back before scooting out to do whatever it was they were doing.

Dez continued our previous conversation as if it hadn't been disrupted. "The bottom line is, most vampires seem to have an inborn knowledge that playing with dead things, truly dead things, is a bad idea. I'm not sure why that's not the case for you, Alex."

"One might assume, Dez, that it's because she's Immortuos." Clio's statement made me grin.

"There is that, hon," I agreed. Dez grunted rather than agree or disagree, so I changed the subject. "I have a theory about our murderer, Clio."

"Do tell." Clio settled herself into a chair, her impossibly long legs folded neatly and modestly.

"It was a mermaid."

"A… mermaid. As in, an ocean dwelling female with the upper half of a human and the lower half of a fish?"

"Well, I don't know if it's exactly like that. It sounds like she looked more human than that. But basically, yes. She lured him to his death. My problem is, mermaids were reputed to lure men to their deaths in water. She came out of the water, but didn't drag him to a watery death. So I'm not sure. But at least it was an idea, and not a stupid one."

"It's a strange one, to be sure. I don't know if mermaids actually exist, though."

Hand it to Clio. She always took my suggestions at face value and considered them, even if they sounded bizarre. "I don't either. But I didn't think vampires existed, and here I am, dead girl walking. And I didn't think zombies existed, and we have one locked in our safe room. So let's say that my ability to suspend my disbelief is being rather expanded, lately."

We heard the doors to the throne room open, and the sound of many feet exiting. The three of us rose and headed toward the entrance to the court. The majority of those exiting were ones I didn't know. I did recognize Cornelius, the voice of the Prince of Toronto. He was as tall and gaunt as ever, and just as imposing. I waved, and he returned it before disappearing into the maze of office hallways beyond.

Clio ushered us ahead of her, and we headed into the dark and cavernous throne room. The usual crowd was notably absent today. Magnus was perched on the edge of his new, more comfortable throne. The worn wooden one he'd used when I first arrived in the city was gone long ago. He was using a laptop on a rolling desk, and motioned us forward as he noted our entry.

"Come sit, friends." He closed the lid of the computer, and settled back in his chair. Clio went up and sat beside him on a smaller chair to his right, while Dez and I pulled up two folding chairs.

We brought Magnus up to date on everything we'd learned about Jim. I went into detail about my magical attempts to lengthen his body's life.

"It sounds as if you've done the right things, Alexandra. I am glad to hear it." He reached out and took Clio's hand, stroking it gently as he talked. "Now we need to deal with the knowledge we have gained about your status in our society."

Dez shifted uncomfortably, and I raised an eyebrow. "Oh?" I wondered if my voice sounded as arched as my brow.

"It was not a light decision when we eradicated the necromancers. They refused to comply with our laws. They acted in the most heinous ways, unethical to the extreme. Even for us. Even for the era in which they lived."

"I'm not them, Magnus." My stomach knotted up, hearing condemnation in his words.

"No, you are not. But you are related to them in a very real way. This disturbs me. It is going to be difficult to explain to some of the city Elders why you are not already dead. I am perhaps more progressive than some of them. I have adapted to the march of time better than many. I still think back to those years, though. It was a terrifying time. They tortured the thralls of our leaders, to gain information. They used their undead minions to blackmail, threaten, and terrorize our families. They did the same to the local religious institutions and clergy. They were hell bent on exposing us to the humans. We did what we thought we had to."

Clio's eyes met mine, and then she looked down. Her face was tight, her words soft. "Alexandra, you have to understand the terror that spread among the vampires at that time. Our thralls were caring for us during the day. At that time, though, the humans very much believed in the magic that we worked. They believed that evil was what sustained us. They hunted us down and killed us when they caught us. It was a time rife with superstition and fear, and not only among the humans."

"So it makes a certain amount of sense to me," I agreed. "But we don't live in a time when people, human people, think we're real. They don't believe in evil beyond their own petty selves, either. They don't hunt us. Superstition is a thing of the past. Unless you have some great fear of the handful of humans that toss salt over their shoulder?"

"It's not today's superstitions that we fear, Alexandra," my Prince replied. "We fear the return of those days of being hunted. Humans aren't superstitious today in the way they used to be, but they're also much more capable of destroying us. Imagine what would happen if one of us were captured. We would be held in a lab and tortured repeatedly, while they learned the best ways to eradicate us."

"A fair fear, and one which I share," I admitted. Dez also nodded. We'd talked about that, late at night when contemplating the idea of bringing some scientists into our vampiric family. "But I'm hardly about to volunteer for that torture, nor am I prone to exposing others. I understand that a couple of years doesn't seem long in your time sense. I have been a good subject to this city and to you for the entire time I have been a member of it, though. That must stand for something!"

"It does. You are sitting here talking, and not incarcerated or dead." Magnus was grim, and his words were blunt. "I don't want to do that to you. I don't believe it necessary. But my beliefs and reality may be at odds. I don't know that your blood, your clan, won't cause you to become what those vampires were, 400 years ago."

"My memories of the times before the purge are not all bad, Alexandra," Clio added. "I've shared some of those tales. I've watched Immortuos mages allow grieving parents to say goodbye to their deceased children. I've watched them raise victims of war to discover important information, to turn the tide of a massacre. I've witnessed them lay dead men to rest, when otherwise they might have continued on as tortured shades, doomed to wander the world insane. There is a very good and humane side to the magic of the necromancers."

"That is what I was trying to do," I said quietly, knowing they could hear me even if I whispered. "I wanted to try and help the poor dead man at my feet. I didn't want to bring him back."

Dez squeezed my thigh. "We know, hon."

"There aren't any writings left from the Immortuos themselves. Those were destroyed at the same time they were. If we look over some of the documentation from Africa and Babylon, we might learn something." Clio smiled at me. "And honestly, the best thing for you to do is to practice. You should have a basic, innate understanding of your own magic. Thus far, every time you've tried something on your own, it has worked. Sometimes it's worked in unexpected ways, but it has worked."

I nodded. "My try at reversing what I did to Jim didn't work, though. And I'm afraid to do much in case I accidentally stop the magic that's holding his body together from rotting. I'm so creeped out over the idea of rotting to death and not being able to get away from it. Ugh!"

"I agree, leaving the poor human to rot is not acceptable," Magnus stated. "But random experimentation isn't good, either. Be sure to do good research before attempting anything. Run your results past Dez before you try anything, Alexandra. Don't give me reason to lock you up."

Just like that, we were dismissed. He waved a hand, and re-opened his laptop. I pressed my lips together into an angry line, but said nothing, and we headed out.

As we left, Clio pulled me away. Magnus and Dez were talking inside the throne room, out of sight and earshot.

"Be quiet about this, Alexandra. Some of the Elders would act rather than think."

"I got that impression," I responded wryly. "I'm not going anywhere. I'll work my ass off at home for the next few nights. I didn't have any other plans, anyhow."

Dez and I headed for home, free to continue figuring out my boundaries and limits. For once, though, Dez was just as in the dark as I was. I have to admit, I was rather keen on the idea that I didn't have to slog through trigonometry lessons anymore. In the immortal worlds of 90s Barbie, "Math is hard!

6 – Down by the Sea

I spent my evening going over the notes I'd made about my work on Jim. I had some ideas on how to de-animate him, but I wasn't willing to experiment on him. I wondered if I should try some experiments on mice or bugs or something, first.

My biggest worries included a) that my magic wasn't working because of outside influences (ie another vampire or supernatural person), b) that I wasn't a necromancer at all and this was a fluke and I'd doomed Jim to be tied to his own corpse for all eternity, and c) that I was a necromancer but not a very good one, and Jim would be doomed. Doooooooom.

On the other hand, I was kind of stoked over the whole thing. I was a necromancer. How cool was that? I mean, okay, I could raise dead things. That was a little off center. Still, I could question dead things, in theory. I could help people who were already dead. Maybe I could be a detective or something! I mean, think about it. Necromancy was the ultimate in recycling, right? I could eat the blood, then re-use the vessel that had once contained it. I wouldn't, mind you. But I could.

Then again, someone out there might want that. Think about it. Someone who's suffered from a horrible disease for their whole life. I could offer them a short while to be with family while they said goodbye the right way, free of pain. I could help out terminal patients who want to remember what it's like to be a functioning human. I could eat them, and then re-animated them to "live" the last few weeks of their lives without drooling on themselves. I could think of hundreds of applications for necromantic magic, and I didn't consider myself all that imaginative.

Alternatively, I might litter the planet with walking, talking corpses and never master the de-animation spell-workings. What then? Would I leave behind Jim and hundreds like him, wandering the world? It would be like one of those zombie movies, but with eloquent, thinking shamblers instead of grunty ones. That would be a Bad Thing.

"Dez?"

"Yeah hon?" He looked up from the pile of papers he was thumbing through on his desk. "What's up?"

"I need to check on Jim, but I don't want to go alone. Will you come with?"

"Yeah, give me a minute." He sorted and stacked, then dusted his hands on his pant legs.

We went to the safe room door together and knocked. I heard a faint sound within, and entered.

It was obvious that Jim was no longer being held together by my magic. The past several hours had left him looking rather bloated again. The stench as we entered was horrid. I frowned, and sprinted to the kitchen and back, returning with another blood bag.

"Let's fix this, Jim. I'm so sorry." I set about getting things organized, and followed the pattern I'd used the previous night. The comforting glow of the blood made me happy. It might not be much, but he was able to hold together for about 24 hours per dose. I could handle doing this. It didn't take much. I wondered if I could pre-load several vials and leave them for timed use, like a prescription. That was for later, though. Right now, I wanted to get this into him.

The results were... well, magical I suppose. His skin took on a considerably less deathly color, and his eyes brightened. I sighed to myself in relief. I needed to figure out a way to extend the time on this if Jim was going to be with us for much longer. Well, if he was going to be with us in any functional way, I corrected myself.

"It helps," Jim stated. "When I drink that stuff, it's like I can think again. When I don't, I can still see and hear and everything, but it's like my ability to interact sort of drops away. It's very frustrating."

"I can't even imagine, Jim. This is a terrible situation. We are working on it from several angles, though, and it will get resolved. I promise."

He nodded. "I appreciate that. I'm feeling out of control, and that's not a comfortable thing. I'm used to being in control of everything."

"I went back to where I found you," I continued, "and I didn't see anything. However, I think we have more information now. Some of our people are checking CCTV cameras in the area to see if your green haired murderess is on them. I'm going to go and talk to people down there tomorrow with a friend of mine, and hopefully that will turn something up. Have you remembered anything else?"

"She was thin, rail thin. Beautiful. Alluring." Jim spoke slowly, articulating each word with care.

"She was naked," Dez reminded him from behind me. "Did you see any tattoos or scars? Any marks that could help us identify her?"

Jim's gaze turned inward as he thought. "I don't remember any. I didn't get a good look at her, though. At first, I didn't notice her, then she was coming out of the water and I was staring at her. At her body, to be honest. And then she was on me." He fell silent. I patted his knee.

"We will bring you justice," I promised. "It's the least we can do."

Dez and I retired for the evening, pausing to shower off the stink of death.

"I need to get in there and re-do that spell before I go out tomorrow night," I commented as I scrubbed Dez's back.

"I agree. I don't want him to liquefy in the safe room. We'd never get the smell out."

"Way to feel for the guy," I complained. "He's the one that's corpsified, not you. Keeping him sustained is pretty much literally the least I can do."

"I know hon. I'm just confused about all of this. Why would a random woman come out of the water and kill this guy? What the heck was he doing down there anyhow? It's not exactly a high class place, as you've pointed out. So much of this smells fishy to me."

"That's probably Jim," I pointed out, grinning. "Seriously, though, I agree. Something isn't quite right. I don't have enough information yet to know what, though. I'm going to call Gabby tonight before bed, and ask her to meet with me. She has that lovely ability to charm humans, which means I can question people without their realizing it. I'm sure she'll help out."

Gabby was one of the first vampires I'd met in Vancouver when I arrived. It was back when I was still all bedraggled and human and fragile. She was elfin in build, short, with wide eyes that always looked surprised. She gave off an aura of innocence that was palpable. She wasn't innocent, though, by any means. She was a vampire, a killer, like myself but moreso. She came across as dainty and helpless, but in action, she was super fast and ridiculously strong. She could disappear from sight in the blink of an eye, even a vampire eye. And she had the power to compel people to do things. On humans it was trivial, and it often worked on vampires as well. She could cause them to answer questions, go places, do things, and then forget everything that had happened. It was a very useful skill, one which I was unable to duplicate using blood magic. I could sometimes erase human memories, and manipulate their feelings and impressions, but could not compel.

Gabby was also mute. She used a combination of sign language and writing to communicate with others. She belonged to a vampire family called the Impotentes, whose members tended to be quite eccentric. Most considered them to be mad, infected with a form of insanity upon being turned into a vampire. They were a very strange family, often choosing to live in squalor and poverty despite not needing to do so. I didn't like most of them, though I considered Gabby to be different. She was almost always clean and pleasant to be around, unlike her family members.

I texted Gabby as I lay in bed waiting for Dez to finish drying off. Need your expertise. Got time tomorrow night to help me out?

Her response was almost immediate. Pick me up at 11pm at court! Excellent.

Dez wandered in from the bathroom, buck naked and still toweling his hair dry. "Is that Gabby?"

"Yep, she told me to pick her up at court tomorrow, early. I'll be up and out at the crack of dusk." I grinned at him. "But for now, it's just me and you, my dear." I eyed his stocky form up and down as if he were a side of beef, and waggled my eyebrows at him.

"Just the two of us, huh?" he asked. He tossed the towel to one side and bounded into the bed beside me. "I suppose we could think up something fun to do."

"You suppose?" I gasped in mock horror. "If I'm not interesting enough for you…"

He growled, springing up to all fours over me. I giggled, screeched happily, and made a half-hearted attempt to escape his nefarious clutches. I flipped onto my belly to try and slither away.

"Oh no you don't!" One of his hands grabbed my ankle, and the other pressed down on my hips, pinning me to the mattress. "You. Are. Mine." Each word was distinct, a sentence unto itself, and as he spoke them he pushed his whole body down over mine. As he spoke the last word, his teeth grazed my shoulder, and I shuddered.

"Bite me!" I hissed. From any human woman, those words would be a sarcastic comment, but from me to my lover, it was an invitation, a mating call, and an acknowledgement that my need met his own. And bite me he did, hard, his sharp fangs slicing into the muscles where my neck and shoulder met.

He groaned into my flesh, the hot taste of my blood in his mouth. He stopped pinning me, instead wrapping his arms and legs around me, trapping me in his embrace. I nuzzled against his arm before sinking my own teeth into his flesh. As the red flood hit my tongue, it felt like I was suddenly high as a kite. My whole body vibrated with the shared passion.

All thoughts of Jim, ladies in lakes, or vampire courts disappeared from our minds. We lost ourselves in one another's bodies, and shared in the intimate bond of blood. When the day sleep overtook us, we lay curled against one another, spent and smiling.

❧

At 10:55pm, I was at court, waiting outside the big doors. I didn't see Clio or Gabby, but that wasn't unusual. I found myself wondering where Magnus slept, considering he always seemed to be here at the court building. With summer daylight restricting our waking time so severely, business had to be packed into the five or so short hours that we could function. Winters, with the 12 and 13 hour long nights, were much preferable. Still, some night was better than no night. I thought about Alaska and how life would be like there, for us, with whole months that the sun never set. Ick.

Gabby slipped from the courtroom a few minutes later, and pranced over to give me a big hug. She wore a pair of baggy overalls with a little bear patch on one knee, and a dark tee shirt sporting a rainbow across the chest. I hugged her back fiercely and smiled.

"Thank you for being willing to help," I said as we walked out of the BC Fisheries building.

She snatched up my hand, allowing her to 'speak' in my mind. *I always like to help you, Alexandra. You're a good person.*

"Why thank you, m'dear." I continued to hold her hand as we crossed the parking lot to my car. "I need to find out some information about a pretty naked girl with green seaweed hair," I explained. She stared at me, head tilted quizzically. I explained in detail as we pulled out of the lot and onto the road that led off Annacis Island and to the mainland. I kept my eyes on the road as I drove, not wanting to see her expression when I revealed that I was a necromancer. I suspected that Gabby was plenty old enough to have seen the original Immortuos eradicated.

You aren't the only one, you know. Her voice resonated in my head. There was no trace of accusation in her mental 'voice', and no sense of concern.

"What?" I almost went off the road with surprise. "But Magnus was clear. All the Immortuos were destroyed back in the early 1600s."

That's correct, Gabby agreed. But it's a spur bloodline, it always has been. It erupts off the Sanguinem line every time. Or it could be the other way around. Hard to tell.

I let that sink in. "How do you know this? Do you know any others like me?" My voice sounded pitiful and eager, even to my own ears.

I do. They hide what they can do. They pretend, blending in as less-abled Sanguinem, or sometimes as Impotentes. They are, after all, under threat of death.

"I'd noticed," I muttered wryly. "Can I meet them? Do they know what they are? How do they learn? Can I learn from them? Would I have to leave Dez?" All the questions came spilling out of me in a rush, as the enormity of Gabby's simple statement sunk in. There were vampires out there like me! I wasn't alone.

It will take time to meet them. They are afraid to know others. They hardly know about one another. I know three besides you, and I had thought maybe you were. None of you are great with the math part, you know. She chuckled, a happy sound. Gabby never got frustrated with my questions and demands for information. If you plan on being openly a necromancer, then you must fight for that right on your own. Only after you have won will the others expose themselves. They are too afraid to come out in the open. None are in current favor with the court. They aren't bold, like you. Most are old, and tired, and ill-equipped to be overturning tradition.

"Hell yes, I plan to fight it. Gabby, I am what I am. Nothing's going to change that. I can't pretend to be something I'm not. And frankly, I can't turn back the clock. Having animated Jim, it's kind of obvious what I am. So yes, I'm going to fight to stand tall as a necromancer."

Gabby nodded vigorously. Good for you! Good girl! From anyone else, that would have sounded patronizing. From Gabby, it was a childish and wholly appropriate expression of agreement. For all her youthful appearance, however, Gabby was anything but innocent. I had seen her take down a vicious she-devil of a vampire with no hesitation or remorse. That exterior belied the instinctual killer within. But today, I was a good girl in her eyes, and I'd take that.

"If it comes down to it, I'll protest for my right to exist and procreate. I never did anything like that when I was alive, but damn it, I will now that I'm dead." I thumped my palm on the steering wheel firmly.

We drove to the mall near the wastewater plant, and parked out back, behind the pub there. Few people were around, and we found a nice, secluded spot beside a dumpster. I locked the car, and the two of us looked around. Gabby motioned for me to wait, and disappeared.

I still had no idea how she did that. One moment she'd be there, and the next, she was completely gone. She might move so fast I couldn't see her, or she might bend light so she was hidden. One guess was as good as the next. Regardless, she could get around without being seen, and she was indeed fast. I was fast, quite a bit faster than Dez, and Gabby could run laps around me as if I were standing still. I assumed she was doing a quick reconnoiter, to make sure no one would see us doing things we ought not be doing. Well, by human standards at least.

As instantly as she'd been gone, she returned. It's all clear. There are a couple of humans down near the pub door. They're very drunk and I don't think they'd see us even if we were walking naked in front of them. I snickered and nodded. We skirted the parking lot and moved into the trees beyond. There was no groomed trail, but the dark didn't hamper us much, and animal paths served as well as sidewalks to our kind. We headed east and south, along the tree line, until we reached the Capilano Trail that led along the river. There we slowed down to more human speeds, linked our arms like the chums we were, and sauntered the silent trail together.

A few minutes later we had reached the bridge where I had found Jim. I showed Gabby exactly where his body had been.

"He was laying here on the pavement. He'd completely bled out by the time I arrived, but there was blood all over the pavement around him." I indicated the size of the puddle he'd been lying in. I was surprised that there were no stains on the ground, and everything had been cleaned up. "From talking to him, it sounds like he came from the east, under the train bridge or maybe the Lion's Gate. Then he made his way down here on foot. When he reached this crossroads, he heard or saw something. When he looked up, a naked woman was coming out of the water."

We both looked out over the river. It wasn't all that wide or deep, and we could have swam across if we'd wanted to. The tide wasn't very high right now, though, and it would have been deeper the night I found him. Surely it wasn't secluded enough for someone to be doing nude swimming here? And it would have been mighty cold, despite the warm weather!

I pointed to a spot to the south of the railway bridge, which seemed to best match the description

Jim had given. "Sounds like she came up right about there. Then she walked onto the rocks here, and came toward him. He says she looked kind of greenish, with wet hair and seaweed in it."

There's some of that green stringy stuff there, Gabby pointed out. Maybe it got caught in her hair when she got out. What then?

"Well, then she came toward him. He described her rather eerily. Said she was short, but her face was long, and her eyes very dark. I felt like he was talking about a character from a video game from the description." I shuddered. "And then she came right up to him and killed him. With her fingernails. Which were like claws."

That sounds really creepy, Gabby commented. She looked around, examining the area thoroughly. It was well lit where we were standing, though darker below the bridge itself. The trail here was well cared for and paved with cement. There were no visible potholes. The garbage cans attached to the light poles were half filled, implying people used them instead of tossing trash to the ground. We knew that they were maintained, because they weren't entirely full. I saw no evidence of drug dealers or other nefarious criminals in the area.

Gabby poked around the railroad tracks, climbing on and around them. She sniffed along the water's edge for a while, from the bridge until far past where Jim's body had been found. We ran into a handful of people the entire time, and Gabby had me question each one. None had seen a girl with green hair, never mind a naked one.

I was unhappy at finding nothing, and frustrated because I'd made no progress. I was fighting a growing sense of dread as we poked about, the pit of my stomach lurching with unease. I couldn't see anything wrong, and I couldn't hear anything wrong. There was no evidence at all, and yet I still struggled with the knowledge that there was something very wrong. I kept hearing the faint strains of a song from far off, which distracted me from my investigations and irritated me.

Gabby and I had finished with a couple we'd unearthed from beneath a bush near the beach, when the Toccata and Fugue in D Minor began to blare out of my pants. As the initial crescendo was reached, I realized it was my phone. Gabby was staring at me.

"What? I like it!" I glared at Gabby as I pulled the cell free of my jeans pocket and answered it. "Yes?"

"You need to come see this, Alexandra," Clio's voice was firm and unquestionable. "I found your green haired hussy."

"You're kidding. That's great! Gabby and I are on our way. Where are you?" Clio shared an address with me, and I plugged it into my GPS. We hightailed it back to the car and headed into the city.

The lights and sounds of the city zipped past my windows as I drove. I loved Vancouver. It was a teeming morass of scents that teased at your nostrils. The people all had their own smells, of course. There was also a tang of seaweed and salt water, of fish, and always of Asian cooking of one type or another. Even in the dead of night, there were humans up and doing things in Vancouver. It was such a wonderful and amazing city.

The GPS directed us to a security company in the heart of the downtown business district. The wide glass doors opened on a marble foyer with modern accents. We took an elevator up, and the doors slid open to reveal a standard reception area. It was all very normal, and very human. I saw Clio standing behind someone working at a desk, and she beckoned to me. Gabby and I went in and straight to her.

"It isn't crystal clear, but this looks to definitely be your girl," Clio said immediately. "George here has been a great help." She patted the grey-suited, somewhat pot-bellied gentleman sitting at the desk.

"Show me what you've got, George." I pulled over one of the chairs from another desk and straddled it backwards.

On the screen was a grainy but decent color image of a paved road with chain link fencing along it. A man I recognized as one of the murder victims wandered on screen, sauntering by. From out of view, a noise or movement distracted him, and he paused. There were some flickers, and then the man was laying on the ground, bleeding. It was pretty gruesome, and I found myself wishing I'd eaten before we came here.

"What are those flickering parts?" I asked. "And where is my green haired hussy?"

"Oh wait," Clio smiled. "Watch."

George rewound the video, fiddled at his keyboard for a moment, and then started it forward, much slower. I saw it this time, and I could tell Gabby and Clio did as well. I'm pretty sure it wasn't slow enough for George to see, yet, but he'd get there. As I waited, he rewound it again, and then played it forward even slower.

Our guy was walking, and he looked off screen. He stopped walking, and then our naked lady sprinted into view. She moved incredibly fast; there was no longer any doubt she was something other than human. No human could move like that. Gabby's eyes were like saucers as she watched, rapt. It was hard to see all her details, both due to the speed she was moving at and the graininess of the image. She had the elongated face, the tiny stature, and the very sea green hair described by Jim. Well I'll be a monkey's uncle. We watched the slowed video, as she stabbed the man several times with what appeared to be knives.

"Can you enhance the picture?" I pointed at the woman in the now-paused video. "I would like to see her."

George cleared his throat. "Um, this isn't a TV show, ma'am," he explained, his voice gruff. "All that stuff about digital enhancement is fictional. I mean, I guess the government could do it, but I sure can't. What you see is what you get."

"Got it. Can you print out a still of this?" I straightened up and stood, putting the chair back.

"I can, and I already have. You can get it from the printer in a minute."

Clio kissed the top of George's head and he blushed. I could almost taste the blood rushing into his face. I had to turn away for a moment as my fangs descended part way. How embarrassing! I walked to the water cooler on the other side of the reception area, and filled a tiny paper cup while thinking about trigonometry. I should have eaten earlier. I pretended to drink the water, poured it into a nearby plant, and then tossed the cup.

As I returned, I pulled the color still off the printer and stared at it. Grainy it might be, but it was definitely our girl. She did actually appear to have a greenish cast to her skin and hair, which surprised me. I had assumed it was a function of the lighting that night, or Jim's dying visions. Nope, it was a real thing. Well, alright then.

"How is it you ladies are all hunting a naked girl?" George asked as we readied ourselves to leave. "How come the cops haven't been by yet?"

"The cops haven't figured out the connection yet, hon," Clio explained in a bland tone. "When they do come by, please don't mention us. It's bad for our business."

George nodded. "That's fine. No one's being hurt by this. Well, except the dead dude. But that wasn't anything to do with you guys. Gals," he corrected himself.

We three let ourselves out, and returned to street level. I tucked the image into my purse.

"What does he think our business is, Clio?" I inquired. Gabby grinned and listened.

"Oh, he thinks I'm a 'private dick'," Clio responded offhandedly.

"A detective for hire? Oh, that's cool!" I chuckled.

"It is," she admitted, a very smug look on her face. "And George is handy. The security company he works for monitors all sorts of off-beat video feeds. Sometimes I can get him to find a needle in a haystack for me. Like tonight."

"Well, that was profitable. Now we have something to go on. However, there's no way I can show this image to humans. That," I stated, patting my purse where the picture was residing, "is most definitely not a human female."

"No, it is not," Clio agreed. "We need to head back to court and go over this with Magnus. I have no idea what she is, but she is not human."

7 – Truth is Stranger Than Fiction

Gabby and I returned to court in my car, while Clio followed in her own. We took the image to Magnus, who stared at it for a very long time.

"This woman is going around killing humans, not vampires," he stated. "She isn't a vampire herself, either. I have no jurisdiction over her."

"That may be true, my Prince, but we can't allow her to go on slaughtering innocents, can we?" I frowned, taking the picture back and stuffing it into my purse once more.

"Her actions may impact our lives here, so no, I can't allow her to take lives willy nilly. Yet I have no idea what she is. She looks human, except…" His voice trailed off to silence.

"That 'except' is very large, Magnus," Clio noted. "She has a humanesque form, but she is not human. On the video feed you could see how fast she moved. The security man had to slow it down for us to see it at all, and even moreso for his human eyes to track it. Her speed rivals Gabby's, and that's saying something."

"Understood. Alexandra, apparently you get your wish one more time. We'll halt our search for ways to dispatch your zombie for a while, until we have dealt with the woman who took his life. Once she is no longer a threat, we'll have to return to the problem of him, but until then he has a reprieve. As do you," he added.

Gabby looked irritated, her mouth pulling into a thin line, her eyes hardening. I processed that for a moment. "My Prince," I said in clipped, formal tones and with a bow and flourish, "I have no wish to earn a reprieve for being myself. I am what I am, and that is something you are going to have to come to terms with. I'm no different now than I was a week ago when you were finding me pleasant and useful company. Your implication to the contrary angers me." I allowed a little of the growl I was feeling inside to creep into my voice.

Magnus scowled at me, his fingers steepled and stiff. "Alexandra, your attitude is out of line." His words and tone were cold. Clio and Gabby were looking back and forth between us. Some of the people in the corners of the room were also drifting closer, watching the exchange.

"No, Magnus, it is not. You have been treating me like a pariah, and I refuse to accept it. I'm not your servant or your thrall, and I will not be treated with anything less than the respect I have earned." I stood before him, ramrod straight, chin held high. Alexandra the human might have bowed and scraped before this powerful man, attempting to appease him and lessen his anger. Alexandra of today wasn't interested in that crap. No one could make me a slave or an outsider.

He stewed there, eyebrows drawn into a fearsome frown. I could have looked around, or backed down. Instead, I continued to stare him down. I did not blink, and I did not break eye contact.

With half an eye to the others in his courtroom, Magnus made an almost silent expression of exasperation. "You have earned respect, yes. You are worthy of that respect. But you are also not in the least knowledgeable about our history, Alexandra. You don't understand what you are, or what you may become."

"You're right, I don't. But I do know that I'm not this thing that you fear, right now. If you plan on punishing people for possibilities, why not lock us all up right now?" I indicated the entire court with a grandiose sweep of my arm. "After all, any one of these vampires might choose to go on a killing spree tomorrow. You yourself might. We are predators, after all."

He pursed his lips, and they became a thin purple line. His pallid face became more white. "Don't play games with me, girl." His tone was dangerous, his eyes flashing with indignation and outrage barely contained.

"I'm not," I said, keeping my voice even and steady. "I don't play games, Magnus. If you haven't figured that out yet, that's your problem. I don't do politics. This is at an end. Fix this, now."

I spun on my heel and marched out of the room, leaving a sputtering and verbally dethroned Prince behind me. I was done with this nonsense. I was not going to allow myself to become some kind of subservient drudge because of an accident of blood. I nursed a momentary concern that Magnus might banish me. I guessed that he was too nervous about my necromancy to actually do that, but who knew? If he had valid concerns about me making a sharp right turn into the Dark Side, he would need to keep me close.

I slammed myself down into the bucket seat of my car and yanked the door closed with a vengeance. I wanted to hit something, but I knew better. All I would do is break the car, and then I'd have to run home, and that would suck. Damn it!

A faint tap at my window made me jump, and I smacked my head against the roof. Swearing, I opened the window to let Gabby hold my hand.

Oh Alex, that was terrifying, how could you do that? She was shivering, either with delight or fear, I couldn't tell. The Prince is so upset! He's shouting at Clio and everyone else, and then he shooed everyone out of the room, and slammed the big doors. Clio is crying, and it's just awful!

"He should have thought about that before he treated me like crap, Gabby. I'm all done with that. I'm going home now." I started to roll the window up after letting go of her hand. She scrabbled to maintain contact, but the glass continued its journey upward, sealing me away from her. I'm sure if she'd wanted to, she could have magically appeared inside the car with me, but she let me be.

❧❧

I arrived home to find Dez waiting in the living room, staring out the glass double doors into the backyard and beyond. He turned as I entered, and watched me toss my keys into the bowl on the table by the door.

"Long day?" he inquired.

"You could say that." I fell onto the sofa, face first, defeated and deflated.

He crouched down beside me and rubbed my back. It felt good, and I sighed. Finally, I sat up, pushing away the tears I didn't want to deal with. Dez handed me a warmed bag of blood, which I ate in silence.

"Clio called while you were on the way home." He sat beside me on the couch, his knee touching mine.

"I'm sure she did. And was she still crying?"

"She didn't sound like she was crying, but she was quite concerned about you. And our illustrious prince was howling something or other in the background."

"I have finally found life, Dez. I'm not giving it up for anyone. Not for Magnus. Not for you, even. It doesn't matter if I'm a blood mage or a necromancer or something else entirely," I murmured, my tone even and steady. I wasn't yelling anymore.

"It sounds like Magnus agrees with that. He is angry, and you defied him in front of his people, but he isn't an idiot. If nothing else, you are the only necromancer in this century, and he'd be stupid to let you go. But more than that, he is your friend and mine."

"He should start acting like it, then." I tossed the now-empty bag on the coffee table, and leaned back, closing my eyes.

"Yes he should," Dez agreed. He took my hand and kissed it with soft and gentle lips. "He'll come around. He is a natural leader, and given sensible and reasonable information, he'll use it and learn from it. But it's going to take a bit of time. He has to fight past ancient prejudices first. That's never easy."

I sucked in a big breath, held it for a count of ten, and let it out. Whether it was necessary for us to breathe or not, it felt good to take deep breaths and exercise the lungs. I opened my eyes and looked at Dez. "We found the girl."

He was surprised. "You did? Clio didn't mention that. That's great! Where is she? Who is she?"

"We haven't found her, in the present tense," I corrected. "We found her on video. Here, this is her." I dug her picture out of my purse and handed it to him. "She really is kind of green."

He studied the image for a long time. "Did Magnus know who or what she was?" He had that intense look on his face, his concentration face.

"Nope, but he was going to look into things." I took the picture back and looked at it again. "You know, I was half joking earlier when I told you and Gabby she was a mermaid. She does kind of look a little watery, though, doesn't she?"

He peered over my shoulder. "Well, yes, but it looks like she just came out of the water. Everyone looks a little watery then. It's a smart tactic, by the way. The water hides any trail that dogs or vampires might follow. It also washes away blood evidence that would lead human police to her. It's a good move, from a predatory point of view."

"You think all her attacks are happening from the water?" I contemplated that one. All the sites were near the water, yes. Could she have a boat she was staying on? Maybe this was a supernatural creature that lived on the water. "It's still pretty cold out there, though."

"To some creatures, yes. Someone like us wouldn't be bothered by it, of course." He was right. My little dip into the water a few days earlier hadn't bothered me in the least.

"She isn't a vampire, though. Even if she moves as fast as us."

"No, she isn't a vampire."

"I want to show this to Jim."

Jim recoiled when he saw the image. It was the most emotion I'd seen him display since I'd raised him.

"That's her," he whispered, voice cracking. "She-" He gagged, shuddered, and looked away.

Dez and I exchanged significant glances.

"Do you remember any of the details of your death?" I prodded. "I know this must be disturbing but we're trying to find out more about her. She's killed others, at least two others we know of."

Jim glared at me. "Do I remember my death? Not really, no. I remember those fingers, like knives, cutting into my soul. Everything goes black after that. I remember the pain, though." Bitterness filled his voice and face, and his shoulders shook as he clenched his hands into fists.

"Is there any reason she has for wanting to kill you? Did you know her when you were alive?" Dez, mindful of Jim's mental state, used his most compassionate and mellow tone. We needed the information.

"I didn't know her, no. I don't recognize her. She was just some girl, that's it." Jim refused to look at us. His nostrils flared, and his lips became a hard, thin line.

"Did you have any enemies? She could be a wife, or a daughter?" I tried to think of any reason at all for this random woman to be attacking Jim and the other men.

"Why would I have enemies? Everyone likes me."

I sighed and gave up for the night. "I want you to think about it today, okay? Any reason she might have had to want to hurt you. Or if you saw her somewhere, before the night she killed you. It might have been a random meeting. A stranger you passed by, even."

"Whatever." Jim lay on his bunk and turned his back to us.

Dez and I retreated, locking the safe room door as we left. We were taking no chances that an angry zombie might escape into the night.

"He's hiding something," Dez said the moment we were out of earshot.

"I know. But I don't know what." I headed to the office, and pulled out the copies I'd made of the police reports on the other murders. The dates were scattered. The first one we knew of was late in February. The second one was two weeks later at the water reclamation plant. Jim's murder was at the train bridge, a full month after the second one. It made no sense.

"There are likely other murders we don't know about, hon." Dez took the files from my hands and laid them on the desk. "There might be a decent pattern to them, if we knew about all of them."

"Or there might be no pattern at all, and we're doing nothing more than pissing in the wind," I countered. "Bottom line is, we're not cops. Having a few supernatural senses doesn't make us detectives. Pretending otherwise would be stupid. We don't have the skills to do this." I shoved the files away from me, and they skittered across the desktop and fell to the ground.

Dez examined me, his eyes critical. "I find it interesting to hear you say that, considering you just told the Prince of Vancouver that he could shove something up his own ass, all corners. No, we are not cops. But we're also not hunting down a fugitive to bring her to justice. We're seeking prey. We are predators. We have all the skills we need for this. What you need is to think about it from a different direction."

I blinked. I had been trying to think about this entire mess like a cop. I'm not sure why, but it was true. I didn't need to think about it like a cop, though, because I wasn't a cop. I was a predator. I wasn't seeking this girl to turn her over to the police. I knew damn well that, if we captured her, she wouldn't make it as far as the car. Whatever information we needed would be extracted, and then we would drain her. If not Dez or myself, then one of the other vampires. We weren't policing the waterfront, we were hunting there.

I pulled out the map of the area and pored over it again. "What if I out-predator the predator?" I mused. I pointed to the three murder locations we knew of. "Here, these are all in a line. Even if they aren't a specific length of time away from one another, they're always close to this shoreline. The paintball place is the farthest away, and it's only about a thousand feet from the water. That's nothing."

"What are you thinking, love?"

"I'm thinking that if I switch my prey to match hers, I might be able to find her next target. Then, if I am patient, I can catch her in the act."

Dez nodded thoughtfully. "Not bad. Out-predator the predator. Now if only you knew why she picked her prey."

"Yeah…"

I spent a few hours researching the three men I knew about. The internet yielded her bounty unto me, but not enough to establish a clear pattern. Each of the men was relatively attractive, and successful in his own way. They were all quiet types, people the neighbors said were almost invisible. Social media and newspaper reports on their deaths revealed all three were passionate when arguing about topics of interest to them, and had high opinions of themselves. One was married, and the other two were not. Two had a death associated with them (a wife, a girlfriend) but the other had not. Two were relatively well off, while the third had recently filed for bankruptcy and was suffering.

I pushed away from my desk, swearing under my breath.

"Problems, hon?" Dez looked up from his own desk, and from the complex symbols he was charting in a notebook.

"No, it's fine. I just had hoped to find more than I did. And now it's time to go to bed and I don't feel like I made any progress."

His heavy chair scraped against the wood floor as he rose to come to me. His arms wrapped around my shoulders, and he stroked my hair with a gentleness that he hid from the rest of the world.

"Let's go to bed then," Dez said, smiling. "Tomorrow is a whole new day, with no mistakes in it. You can apply yourself to it fresh."

I nodded wordlessly in agreement, and let him draw me out of the office and to bed.

❧❧

The next evening, I woke early. It was rare that I rose before Dez, and I lay beside him in our huge, coffin shaped bed. We didn't move when the day sleep took us, so if we were embracing when it happened, we woke up the same way. His arms were slack around me, and I could have squirmed free without any difficulty. Instead, I enjoyed the closeness. There was no breathing to observe, no snoring to deal with. His skin didn't feel cool to me, though I knew it was about room temperature.

I thought about my night. I wanted to figure out how this woman was picking her prey. I snuggled deeper into Dez's arms while I contemplated the facts.

She hunted men. We'd seen no evidence of hunting women. That meant I couldn't use myself as bait, but that was fine. She hunted men who were successful and comfortable, if not well off. And ones who visited the waterfront. So I had to go looking for late night joggers, perhaps? Why had these men, who lived at random places throughout the city, been walking at that part of the waterfront?

Dez's grasp tightened without warning, and he licked the back of my neck, causing me to squeal.

"Ew, don't do that!" I struggled to get free, giggling. "You are gross!"

He held on, arms unyielding. My own arms were trapped under his, and I was helpless. "I will do as I please, because you're mine," he growled into my ear. This caused me to wriggle even more, ineffective though it was. He began to kiss me all over, nipping at me with his fangs. My cries of protest turned to moans of ecstasy. We spent a while together remembering how much we loved one another.

Some time later, as we were cleaning up and brushing teeth, Dez turned to me. "What were you thinking of, right before I licked you?"

"Hm?" I paused, thinking back as I rinsed my mouth free of toothpaste. "Oh! I was wondering why those guys were all walking on the trail at that time of night. They were all killed at night, and all along that trail between the railway bridge and the Lion's Gate Bridge. It's an odd place to be walking in the middle of the night, if you're human."

"Yes it is," he agreed. "And what conclusion did you come to?"

"I didn't. You licked me." I grinned, and kissed his arm as I passed him on my way to my bedroom to pick out clothing for the night. "But I'm working on it," I called back over my shoulder, as I bounded up the steps to the main floor.

My clothes closet was a massive and pretty obscene affair. In my past, I'd had smaller apartments, back when I was human. When I'd first arrived on Dez's doorstep, I'd had a handful of things in there, but it was almost bare. These days, it was stuffed with all manner of dresses, pants, suits, shirts, shoes, and other paraphernalia. I mulled over my choices while I thought about why those men were found where they were found.

Why did one go walking at the waterfront? Well, for me it was a way to feed without drama. I could always find someone down there. Okay, so why were all those people down there when I was looking for a meal? Why did I seek prey there? They were party people, the ones I usually fed on. A sip here and a nibble there didn't amount to much for them, and I usually didn't have to hunt them down. They came to me.

They came to me. That's how she was picking her prey. There wasn't a pattern because she was hunting a place, not a person. The epiphany hit me like a freight train.

I decided to dress in something provocative. It could be that our merry murderess was luring in her prey by eroticism. The nudity might be distracting her victims, giving her the chance to get close enough to stab them. Being that close to them, the first strike made in the right place would incapacitate them. Death would be swift.

I chose my outfit with precision, designed to attract the human male. I slipped into a jean skirt short enough that bending over would reveal all my assets. I paired it with a burgundy sleeveless blouse that could have doubled as a bikini top if it weren't for the little bit of fringe coming off it. I picked out a pair of three inch heels to match my top, and a small clutch bag to toss my phone and wallet into.

I looked at myself in the mirror in my closet, critical of what I saw. I looked very different from the scared, dumpy human woman who'd arrived in Vancouver only two years or so ago. I was more confident, and more willing to try new things. I didn't shy away from excitement. The knowledge that I was less likely to be injured led me to be more adventurous. In my previous life, anything over an inch of heel would have sent me stumbling and falling over. These days, I could navigate with heels on almost as well as the average human, which was a big deal considering the deficit I'd started with. Of course, I didn't match Clio. She could chase down a burly bodyguard while wearing six inch spiked heels, and not break a sweat (or a heel). Honestly, the woman was terrifying.

I heard a low wolf whistle behind me, and turned to see Dez standing in my doorway. His hungry gaze traveled up and down my body, and I smirked.

"Dress for the job you want, they always say. I want to catch a predator. Think this will do?" I struck a pose, hand on hip.

"You'll sure catch something, in that get-up. If you were human, I'd be worried for your safety. As it is, I'm worried for the safety of any males in your vicinity. Damn, you are fine." He crossed the space between us in an instant, and pulled me into a passionate kiss.

"Unf," I commented, as he let me go and stepped back to drink in the sight of me once more. "Is it a bit over the top?"

"No, I think it's just right. Go, fly, eat up the night, my darling." He grinned saucily at me, patted my posterior, and went off to his office to work.

8 – Sorrow and Horror

I strolled along the Capilano Pacific Trail, enjoying the views. It was a Saturday night and there were humans thronging the beach despite the 50° F weather. There was alcohol and debauchery, much of it in plain sight. I had parked my car at the west end of Ambleside Beach, and was making slow progress eastward. The lights of the Lion's Gate Bridge glittered in the distance, rainbow hues shimmering over the water. My ultimate destination for the evening lay only a few hundred feet beyond its bright, busy bulk.

Dez had been right about my attracting attention. My usual method of hunting was to dress down, hide in the crowd. I wasn't prone to grandstanding. My current outfit (or lack thereof) had attracted quite a few male gazes, and some female ones, too. I strutted along with a pronounced wiggle, 'dat ass' swaying provocatively.

My prey hunted her prey here. Most male prey was attracted by feminine wiles, in my experience. A couple of very young men peeled off their pack of friends to give me a try, but I brushed them off. They didn't fit the image that I thought would match what the woman was after. They were too young, insecure. They didn't hold the self-confidence of the previous victims. I was looking for her victims, not my own. Where I wanted young and inexperienced, with hot blood, she was looking for a slower burn, more maturity. At least I hoped I had that right.

It didn't take long to reach the end of Ambleside Beach, even without cheating and using my unnatural speed. I made the walk last over an hour, moving as if distracted by occasional texts on my phone. I watched all the delicious young people cavorting in the sand and water, scanning each one. The waterfront was dotted with fires here and there, until the end of the main beach. The dog beach was almost deserted. There were only two women walking their pets together, chatting and giggling together.

I scanned ahead on the trail, beyond the sandy beach and up closer to where I'd found Jim. It was obscured on one side by trees and bushes, as the trail curved northward up ahead. I could smell at least one human up there, though. The wind was blowing toward me, and the scent of musky maleness drifted down. I continued my stroll, doing my utmost to appear oblivious to the world around me. I pulled out my phone and texted an order to my favorite Mexican place. I made sure to type with two thumbs, slow going even by human standards, while not looking around.

Of course, I didn't need to look around that much. I was more aware of my surroundings than humans in general. I could smell and feel much more than the average human being, and my hearing was far superior. I could glance up for the briefest of moments, unnoticeable to a human, and see and remember everything in front of me.

I knew he was there before he saw me. His breathing was even, measured, but his heart was beating fast. He had picked a spot that was dark, and only a little off the trail. The trees there dipped low, making a natural arch, and the light above the area was out. It was an adequate place to ambush a woman, especially when the tide was high, as it was now. The water lapped right up to the stone edge of the cement path tonight. It gave me very little room to run away or get to a more lighted spot. The next light was the one under which I'd found Jim's body. That was a full 200 feet ahead and around the last curve of the path before the railway bridge.

I got almost to the place where he was sure to jump me, but not quite, and bent down to fix the strap on my heels. I fiddled with it, giving him time to build his resolve, and listened to the strong heartbeat pounding against his rib cage. He was sure of himself, but I wasn't in quite the right place. I centered myself. I focused on that steady and fast thumping that was so loud to my sensitive ears, and then I heard another sound.

It was music, maybe? I couldn't be sure. It was something, a sound, a voice perhaps, niggling away at the back of my brain. I stood up, ready to walk forward, my nerves taut. I was beyond surprised when my gentleman thug stepped haltingly out of the shadows. He walked past me as if blind, and stumbled over the edge of the little path wall and into the water.

I blinked. What the hell? Meanwhile, my brain itched from whatever that almost-sound was. I growled, and ditched my heels and purse under the bush my erstwhile attacker had abandoned, and went after him.

That's when she rose up out of the water. I had missed the little trails in the moonlit bay, but he hadn't. He stood there, mouth gaping, his slacks soaking up the salt water like a wick. I halted, staring at this distinctly green tinged, naked woman rising up. The water streamed off her almost luminous skin like a selkie shedding its coat.

"Leave him alone. You deal with me!" I called out. I tried to be loud enough for her to hear me but quiet enough to not travel beyond where we stood. She looked at me finally, her dark eyes inhuman and quite terrifying. I reminded myself that I was a strong and capable killing machine. I didn't need to be afraid of strange green women in lakes, right? My brain refused to take the hint.

She said nothing, and once she'd assessed me as not a threat, she moved toward him again. The dimwit just stood there, ignoring the terror in front of him. He ignored everything but her, even the water that squelched in his shoes.

"Dude!" I hissed. "Move!" I touched his shoulder, but he didn't react at all. It was as if he was moving in slow motion, almost rooted to the spot. She was moving at a normal pace. Well, as normal as you could be when wading naked through hip deep water toward someone in knee deep water. I checked my own perceptions. It occurred to me that I might be watching in 'fast motion' as I sometimes did when Gabby was moving fast. I was not, however.

I shuffled forward, careful of my footing in the cool water, and put myself between the woman and the man. "Stop!" I held up my hand, blocking her.

"No," she whispered, a vocalization that was somewhere between a moan and a sob. My soul shriveled away from it, and it took my whole will to stand there and not move.

"I'm not letting you kill another innocent man," I said, quiet and firm. "No more. This is over!"

"No," she moaned again, soft and sibilant. "Not innocent, not innocent…" Her voice faded, like wind dissipating in the trees.

"What are you?" I asked, unable to stop myself. She very obviously wasn't human. I snapped a couple of pictures of her with my phone, which was still in my hand. I stashed the phone in the cup of my bra, and splashed forward another step.

"Murdered… left… decayed…" I could hear her words, but she wasn't making any sense.

"Wait, you were murdered? Are you a ghost?" I hadn't ever met a ghost before, but that didn't mean anything. I had learned in the vampire community that many of the myths and legends were based on the truth.

"Murdered," she agreed, and looked past me to the man. A look of frustration crossed her face and she reached out toward him. My brain itch flared back into existence. The man whimpered, a pitiful sound, and shuffled forward as if through quicksand. I was in the way, but he didn't see me. He pushed against me in his attempt to get to her.

"You can't murder this man," I said firmly. I whirled around and slapped him hard across the face. He shuddered, and I'm sure his ears were ringing from the blow. He staggered back two steps, then seemed to awaken from his walking slumber.

"What the fuck?" he asked, bewildered. He backed away several paces, and then turned and waded out of the water. He disappeared down the path that skirted the nearby golf course. I turned back to my green girl.

"What are you?" I repeated.

"Dead. I am dead. Murdered, left to drift, to decay, to disappear." She moved away from me, deeper into the water, her long hair drifting around her.

I burst forward, using all the speed at my disposal, and snatched at her wrist. My fingers held fast for a second or two, and then passed through her like she was mist. Indeed, like mist, she seemed to break up and dissipate over the water as I watched.

"Damn it!" I swore, sloshing back to the path. I snatched up my heels and purse from their bush. I pushed into the low tree line, then picked up speed. I wouldn't be seen here, and under the cover of the darkness of the night and the shade of the trees, no one would notice. I sprinted back to my car, and on to Magnus and Clio, and the court, and its library.

At the BC Fisheries building, I screeched to a halt, my car not even within the lines of the parking spot I'd chosen. I sped into the building, ignoring the elevator in favor of the stairs. I pounded up them, still somewhat damp. My shoes were abandoned in the car, but my phone was still tucked into my bra. I arrived at the huge double doors and announced myself, breathless.

Clio opened the doors, expecting someone else, I guessed. Her face registered surprise. Then she noted my sexy outfit stained with salt water, my bare feet, and general state of dishevelment.

"Come in," she ordered, and took my hand and drew me up to the throne. Magnus was deep in conversation with his father, discussing finances, I was sure. Vancouver was a costly place to be Prince. When he and Dario saw me, though, they dropped what they were doing and Magnus waved me forward.

"I saw her," I stated without waiting. "She's not human. Not vampire. Maybe some kind of water spirit?"

I went over the events of the night in great detail for Magnus and everyone else present. I left out nothing, including the claim that she had been murdered. I explained the brain itch, as well as my concern that she was somehow compelling the men she was preying upon.

"He didn't have a chance. Once he saw her, it was like he was drawn to her. I mean, I was dressed as total eye candy, and that perp was about to snack on me. Then she came up out of the water and from that moment on, I didn't exist anymore. He was completely focused on her."

Clio had pulled the laptop to her, and was typing a staccato beat while I spoke.

I went on. "If I hadn't literally stood between them, he would have walked out into that water and drowned."

"About that," Magnus interrupted. "We intercepted coroner reports about your male victims. Their causes of death was stabbing, but there was water in the lungs. I'm guessing your walking corpse may be the same."

"Huh. I guess it makes sense. She lures them to the water, then incapacitates them, and drags them to land to stab them?" I had meant it as a statement, but as I said it, it came out as more of a question. That didn't make sense at all, despite what I'd just said. We'd seen the one attack on video, and she didn't take the victim anywhere near the water. She knifed him and left him there.

"At least one of your vics wasn't ever that near to the water. She must have come out." Magnus pursed his lips, one long, manicured finger tapping against the side of his nose as he thought. "I suppose it might be a form of magic that holds them enthralled."

"That is reasonable," Clio chimed, as she continued to type rapidly. "You've always been sensitive to various powers, Alexandra. Remember how you felt when you first arrived here, before you were even turned."

I thought back to that night, only a couple of years ago but feeling like so much longer. I'd been human, with dull senses and a complete lack of the seriousness of my own situation. Someone had been messing around, attempting to use a vampiric power on me. It had caused an unholy buzzing in my brain pan that almost drove me insane. It still did, though I could sort of tune it out if I needed to, these days. Not every power set it off; some of the passive ones didn't register at all. Gabby's powers of speed and her ability to speak to me were both examples of ones that didn't set me off. Blood magic created a minuscule background sensation that wasn't unpleasant. Compelling powers, though, tended to make me feel like I had a hive of angry bees swarming inside my head.

"You think the itchy brain was because of whatever power she was using?" I could see how that might be. I'd never felt it quite like that before, but I also hadn't ever seen whatever that woman was, before, either. "So she was using some kind of power to compel her victims to come to her, or to hold still, then."

Magnus nodded. "It looks that way."

"Capturing her is not going to be easy, if that's what we decide to do," I noted. "When I grabbed her, she sort of became not solid."

"That's sounds unusual," Magnus stated. "I've never heard of anything that can dissolve itself."

"She didn't dissolve. It was more like she turned into mist or something. She… vaporized, I guess." I shrugged, angry at feeling helpless. "One moment I had her by the bony wrist, and the next, my hand was empty and she was gone. Not even a splash."

"Tomorrow night, I want to talk to you and Dez and your corpse." Magnus irritated me by refusing to say Jim's name. "I had thought of bringing the court to you, however it occurs to me that you will need to take it down to the water. You'll want to see if you can smoke out this creature. Come here first, and then you may take it to see if you can figure this mess out."

The phrasing Magnus used in that last statement made me remember that I was irritated with him. "I will bring Jim here tomorrow if you wish. But only if you promise me that you'll act with at least a modicum of respect," I stated.

Clio's typing stopped, leaving a silent void, and every eye turned until everyone in the room was looking at us.

"And what do you consider to be 'a modicum of respect'," Magnus asked, voice tight.

"Well, you could try using Jim's name, and referring to him as 'him' and not 'it'. I could live with that, to be honest."

Magnus closed his eyes and counted to ten in more than one language. "I hear you. I will endeavor to be a bit more polite around your c- Jim."

I nodded. "Thank you." I wanted to snark at him, but that wasn't going to be any use, so I was polite instead. You catch more flies with honey, after all.

"Before you go, hon, can you give me a better description of this woman?" Clio had paused in her typing once more to look at me.

"I can do you one better," I replied. "I have pictures. Or at least I think I do." I pulled my cell out and flipped open the photo app. There, I found that I had managed to get several blurry and two decent photographs of the woman.

"You can see that Jim's description was pretty accurate," I noted. "She's definitely green, which surprised me. I had thought it was a trick of the light. Nope. She's green. And there was, indeed, seaweed in her hair. She's ridiculously thin, and her face is quite elongated. Her eyes aren't as black as all the images seem to imply, though. They're dark, and sunken, but not as pictured. The photos make her look like her whole upper face is sunken in, and that wasn't the case. They looked like they were bruised or she was incredibly sleep deprived or something."

The three of them pored over the images, and then Clio took copies for herself. "I'll use these to enhance my search. I'm going through modern notations looking for other instances of this kind of thing. I'm also searching among the ancient folklore. If she's supernatural, which appears to be the case, the legends might give up more information than current event news." She smiled, and patted my hand. "Thank you for these. I'm sorry there wasn't more resolution for you, though."

"It's okay. I'm dealing. I'm going home now. I need to buff up Jim so he doesn't lose cohesion before tomorrow, and I need to look into some ancient history myself. Speaking of that, Magnus, may I use your library for a bit?"

"You may. Books about the execution of the necromancers are in the section on Italian history. We talk about the deaths that happened in England the most, because they were recorded by monks. It didn't start there, though; it began in Italy. I suspect the information you get from those histories will be more useful to you." Magnus spoke quietly, and I realized this was an olive branch. He could have denied me entry to the library, or said nothing there was relevant to my inquiry. Instead, he was aiding my quest for information about my current situation. I reset the mad flag for him; he was trying, and now I needed to do so as well.

"Thank you, my Prince. It is greatly appreciated. I am doing everything I can to be an asset and good citizen of your city."

"I know you are, Alexandra. And while I am concerned, gravely, I do realize you are not those evil people. And I am not who I was then, either."

I bowed in gratitude, and moved past the throne room and into the offices beyond. The private boardroom led into a large double room that contained books and scrolls of various types. Some were kept in special cases, climate controlled so they did not decay. Others were copies of copies, and in better condition, sitting on shelves. I walked the aisles, looking for the Italian history section.

I finally found it, 914.5; apparently vampires also used the Dewey Decimal System for filing their books. I grinned to myself, and ran my finger along the shelf, looking at the titles. There were books on Medici, and books on Italian Renaissance. I found books on the history of government in Italy during the medieval period. I found dozens of books that I could have picked up on Amazon. I wasn't looking for books that were modern, though. As I walked down the aisle, the books got older and more fragile. They went from more modern bindings to hand bound books.

I finally found a series of small, hand sewn books entitled, "On the Eradication of Evil" by Bentto Cavatta. They were written in another language that I guessed was Italian or Latin. The letters were so tiny that I didn't know if I could copy them. I wondered if Google Translate was going to be able to help with this one.

I packed the books up in a travel pouch, waterproof and sealed, and headed back home. I would look through the information tonight and tomorrow evening. Perhaps Dez spoke Italian? I'd have to see.

Dez greeted me at the door. "Jim is not doing well," he informed me immediately. I put the packet of books on the living room couch and headed to the kitchen to grab more blood. I noted that our stores were quite depleted, and jotted a note for Matias, asking him to procure more.

"Let's go deal with this right away," I said, "and I'll catch you up on the rest afterward." Dez nodded, following me out onto the covered porch and down the outside stairs to the lower level. I let myself into the house through the double doors there, and knocked at the safe room door. There was no response.

When I entered, I could see immediately that Jim was suffering. He was lying on the cot, not moving. He looked quite bloated, and the smell was very strong. I shooed a few flies away from him as I approached him, and noted that he appeared to be stiffening.

"I think it's rigor mortis," Dez said in my ear. "You're retarding the decaying process, but not halting it. This usually happens a few hours after death."

I sighed to myself, and settled on a folding card chair to work some magic. First, I infused the bag of blood with energy. I concentrated on stasis, on the idea of the body remaining as it was, stopped. I added the idea of allowing the soul to continue to thrive. A thin sheen of crimson tinged sweat covered me by the end of it, testament to my efforts. To my credit, the glowing bag of blood lay pulsing in my hand for all the world like a beating heart.

"Come on, Jim, let's get some of this into you." I popped the cap out of one of the IV holes, and let a trickle of the energized blood flow into his gaping mouth. His eyes, which were wide with fear, closed as the spell infused him. His stiff arms slowly (too slowly) released from the rigor he'd been trapped in. More able to move, he drank the remainder of the spelled contents with a kind of disgusted eagerness.

Dez patted my shoulder, nodded toward the door, and slipped out. I stayed for a bit, easing Jim into a sitting position. It was almost impressive, watching the decay reverse. It didn't disappear, but it did wind its way back a bit. The bloating went down as I watched. The rigor disappeared entirely. If I weren't so worried about Jim's mental state at the moment, I'd have been darned impressed with my own command of magic.

"Please, let me die," he whispered, his eyes flitting from side to side in a panicked motion. "I can't be like that. I can't do it. I can't!" He grasped my arm, voice shaking with emotion.

"I'm trying, Jim. I promise, I am doing everything I can. I'm not giving up, and we have many people working on helping you."

"If you can spell that stuff to keep me going, why not spell it to stop me, let me go away?"

"I wish it were that easy," I frowned. "But I found your lady. I saw her today. I'll be dealing with her tomorrow. Tomorrow, you need to come with me and Dez to our court. Then we'll head out to where I saw her, near where you died. Tomorrow, Jim. I think we'll see some resolution tomorrow."

"Please…" He cried, quietly, tearlessly.

It broke my heart to leave him, but what more could I do? My sitting there with him wasn't going to fix anything. I needed to look through the books I'd brought home. I needed to learn more, so that I could do whatever it was my ancestors did, to release the souls of the dead.

9 – Revile Revealed

I retrieved the books from my couch, and took them to the office, where Dez had retreated after leaving me. I put the packet on his desk, and laid them out with great care.

"This has to do with the eradication of the necromancers," I said. "Or so I guess. The only problem is that it isn't in English. I don't read Italian. Or Latin. Or whatever this is."

Dez pulled one of the little chapbooks over to him, and flipped through it, heedful of the delicacy of the papers. "I don't think this is straight Italian, love. It looks to me like it's Venetian."

"Venetian is a type of Italian, though, right?" I pulled another of the tiny books out and opened it. "It looks kind of like Italian."

"Yes and no. Venetian is related to Italian. People who speak one can understand many words of the other. A contemporary speaker of Italian language is not going to get it, though. How could he understand the writings of a long-dead vampire who thought and wrote as a native?"

I made a frustrated noise. "Why must this be so damn difficult?" I asked, whining a bit.

"What, you wanted ancient Venetians to write in English?" Dez grinned at me. "Let's feed it into the computer and see what it will do."

I took careful pictures of a few pages with my phone, and sent it to a translation application that we used. It was limited in its scope, but I was hoping it would be able to give us an idea of what was said in the books. After a few moments, it had parsed the copied pages into text, which I fed into the Google translate program.

"I used to sit human my mother I'd go and spend the money in dignity and money. I gave her a prayer and prayer and she helped me and I joined the spirit of Friar." I read that translation out loud and sighed. That made less than no sense.

Dez laughed, and I made a face at him. "It's a program designed for modern languages, my dear. It is a bit limited. I suspect we'll need to pull on an expert for this sort of thing. Did you check with Clio to see if she spoke it?"

"No, but I can ask her."

I paged Clio, Magnus, Gabby, and a handful of other vampires I knew who were older than Dez and myself. I hoped that one or more of them spoke early Renaissance Italian or Venetian. Clio and Magnus responded immediately in the negative. The others were slow getting back to me.

"I'm so frustrated, Dez. I had her in my hands. Literally!" I growled to myself, and fiddled with the bedraggled hem of my jean skirt. "I don't understand any of this."

"It will get better, Alexandra. It takes time to master new skills. You can't learn to be something new overnight, you know. It takes practice, and trial and error. You've been doing a good job of learning magic on your own, and I'll be honest, right now I'm rather relieved. I was beginning to doubt my own ability to teach. You were having such a difficult time with even simple things, things the others picked up in hours. The problem wasn't me or you, it's that you weren't made to do my kind of magic. You can't judge a fish by its ability to ride a bicycle, after all."

"It's easy for you. You have others to turn to, formulae and books and stuff that describe much of what you do. Me, I'm running blind here. It's great that I've figured out some stuff on my own. But before, I knew that I could pull on the knowledge you and the others have. Now I'm facing the idea that I'm going to have to do this all on my own. I have to reinvent the wheel. Alone."

"It's frustrating, I know. But you are an intelligent, articulate woman, Alexandra. You will master this in short order."

I made a non-committal noise. "I'm going to shower."

Showering was my go-to for when I was down. I could stay under the water for a long time, not having to breathe even. It was nice. I could set the water quite hot, and it felt good on my skin. It warmed me, made me feel almost human again.

Not that I wanted to go back to being human. My existence now was wonderful, miles better than my human life. I loved Dez with all my heart, and I loved our life together. There were moments that left me angry, here and there, and this was one of them. I'd get over it, but first I wanted to wallow in it a bit.

I tossed my salt crusted clothing into a pile in the corner, and stepped into the enormous shower. The water came out cold at first, but it didn't have the same effect on me these days as it used to when I was alive. I registered the change in temperature, but it wasn't disturbing or discomforting. I did like it much better once it warmed up, though, at least from a psychological point of view.

I washed my hair, taking my time. I scrubbed it with a mint shampoo, then conditioned it and let it sit. I wasn't sure what magic kept my hair so silky, but death certainly seemed to make for awesome hair and nails, for me. When I rinsed, I used my fingers to smooth out the handful of tangles. It didn't take much, due to it still being quite short.

I scoured the rest of my body with a loofah and my favorite lye soap that smelled of red wine and leather. It didn't hurt, though at one time it might have. It was sensation, and that was enough. I was rinsing the last of the soap from my hands and arms when Dez let himself in and joined me.

Dez didn't understand my fascination with bathing. Vampires didn't get dirty in the same way that humans did, he had explained to me several times. We didn't sweat, for the most part, and we didn't smell. We were inert. But I always showered each day, or took a bath. I liked my bubbles, and my soaps and stinky things. They made me happy. That was enough for Dez, and he would scrub my back for me for the sheer sybaritic pleasure of it.

Today, as it often did, it led to love making. There was something glorious about finally being able to do some of those silly porn movie moves. I wasn't breakable and neither was he, and we were both strong and flexible enough to enjoy it. I wondered if there was vampire porn out there, and it made me giggle.

"What, this is funny?" Dez paused in what he was doing. My back slid to a halt on the glass of the shower enclosure with an embarrassingly loud squeaking noise.

"No, I was just thinking about vampire porn," I grinned, and ran my fingers through his wet hair. The water had become icy cold ages ago, but we didn't care. The chill wasn't noticeable.

"What about it?" Dez continued on with his motions, distracting me.

"Well, I mean, what would it entail?" I envisioned biting and blood, which mixed well with what Dez was doing, and I kissed him quite thoroughly.

He flicked off the water and carried me through to our bed, tossing me onto it. I thanked the good, Amish construction of the bed frame for the umpteenth time. The two of us got lost in sensations for a while. An hour later, as we lay satiated and naked together, Dez answered, "Well, really it's much the same thing as for humans."

"What?" I'd lost track of the earlier conversation and had no idea what he was talking about.

"Vampire porn. You asked about it earlier. Vampire porn is much like regular porn that humans do. It's just that we don't get tired, and have better stamina." He waggled his eyebrows at me, and I giggled.

"Like you know so much about vampire porn," I teased. Dez was so serious sometimes. Then in unguarded moments like this, he could be completely hilarious.

"I do know about vampire porn," he said firmly. He rolled onto his side and leaned on one hand, looking at me. "I don't know that they do it so much these days, but in the '80s, there were a lot of vampires into porn. The whole goth scene was huge, and we really did fit the bill."

"We?" I asked, arching one eyebrow. "Are you telling me you were in porn?"

"I am neither confirming nor denying that statement," he said in a monotone voice. Then he snickered and grabbed my foot, sucking on one of my toes.

"Ew, oh my gawd, Dez, stop!" I pulled at my foot, trying to unlatch him from it. It tickled!

"Not a foot fetishist then, eh?" He let my foot go, and planted a gentle kiss on the curve of my calf. "In any case, sometime when we aren't dealing with dead guys in the safe room and water women in the bay, I'll show you a video."

"Oh good grief," I groaned. "You have copies of old porn?"

"That's enough of that, little girl," he snarled, grinning maniacally. He snatched my leg again and pulled me to him, pushing me over his knee without ceremony. He began spanking me, his rather large hand coming down hard on my bare buttocks.

It devolved quickly at that point. When the sun came up, we were tangled in the bed sheets, curled around one another, smiling.

❧❧

I started my night by refreshing the spells on Jim.

"I am feeling okay," he ventured.

"Yes, but I'm making certain you're as comfortable as you can be. It's not my desire to make you unhappy in any way. I feel horrible about this whole thing."

"I appreciate your efforts. Most women wouldn't go out of their way to make me this comfortable in such trying circumstances."

I patted his arm, feeling awkward, then handed him the bespelled blood to drink. He was looking alright this evening, which was good. There had been no degradation over the day My spells seemed to be holding, this time. "I am doing everything in my power to resolve this. But moreso, I need you to go out with us tonight. The Prince has asked us to bring you to him. You'll be accompanying us."

Jim nodded, eyes not meeting mine. "I don't suppose you have any fresh clothes I could change into?"

I realized with a start that he was still in the same clothing we'd put him into when he arrived several days earlier. "Oh, hon, I'm so sorry! I'll make sure you get clean clothes and a chance to shower if you'd like."

"Thank you."

I hurried out of the safe room and up the stairs to my own bedroom. On the way, I asked one of the servants to pick out more clothing for Jim, of a nicer variety. Then I picked out my own outfit for the night, a nice pair of slacks and a scoop neck top in shimmering blue. I was so glad for being blonde; I had such a wide array of colors I could wear. Anything in jewel tones would work. I slipped into a pair of comfortable, low heeled sandals, and grabbed my purse. Seconds later, I zoomed back downstairs again.

I met Dez coming out of the bedroom, combing his hair. He was in a slate grey suit with royal blue tie and sapphire cufflinks. I skidded to a halt and stared, licking my lips at the sight in front of me.

"Well, don't you clean up nice?" I asked archly, grinning.

"Why yes, I do," he replied, showing his teeth and returning my grin. "But I packed up a pair of shorts and a beach tee in case we end up at Ambleside later. You may want to do the same. It pays to blend in."

"Oh." I hadn't thought of that. I sighed, and sprinted back up to pack a bag with appropriate beach wear. It wouldn't do to be down there in a suit, after all. We didn't like to stand out in that way. It was okay to be "the sexy chick I saw". Being "the short blonde in a suit, who was very out of place" was a whole other thing. After I packed my beach bag, I stopped in the office to pick up my little Italian booklets. I ran my fingers over their fading covers, then slid them into their holder with care.

When I returned, Dez was holding the door of the safe room open for Jim. Jim was looking much better, in a pair of khakis and a golf shirt. One of the servants had found a pair of black sneakers in his size, too. He wasn't as dashing as Dez, but at least he was clean and dressed. I was happy. He looked a bit more animated than he'd been most of the week. It could have been my magic, but it also might have been the prospect of being out of that room, too.

I led the way to the garage, through the causeway. Dez contemplated the two vehicles, then chose my jeep to drive. He slid into the driver's seat, to my surprise. I shrugged, then helped Jim into the backseat where he'd been the night I brought him home. I got in the front passenger side, and buckled up.

"The drive isn't too long," I said, talking toward the back so Jim could hear me and be included in the conversation. "Court isn't all that interesting, but we're hoping to get the answers to a lot of our questions while there."

Jim made a grunting noise behind me. I twisted in my seat to see him staring out the window, a listless look in his eye.

"Are you okay?" I asked him. I had thought he'd be a bit more perked up, being out of the room and the house.

He turned to look at me, eyes blank, face slack. "Sure. I'm dead, and animated. I'm wearing someone else's clothing. I stiffen up at random moments, which is painful and completely terrifying. I didn't ask for any of this. I'm fine, just fine. This is fine." His voice was flat and emotionless as he said it, and I winced.

I turned back to the front of the car and whispered, "Sorry..." Dez snaked his hand across the space between us, and grabbed mine, squeezing it.

The rest of the drive was silent. I didn't even turn on the radio, an unusual thing. I sat there, wondering and pondering. What would happen to Jim if I didn't get this spell reversed? Would he continue like this? Would I need to refresh the magic twice a day, every day, for the rest of eternity? Would we need to keep him locked up in our safe room? I hated not knowing the answers.

Arriving at court was fun. Okay, I'm lying; it was horrid. Anselem, the insufferable pouf, stopped us as we went in. His whole face screwed up into a caricature of himself. I swear to God, he pulled out a lacy white hankie and put it over his nose.

"What is that thing?" he demanded, wafting air away from himself.

Dez started to answer but I walked up to Anselem and raised one eyebrow into a fine, high arch. "This is Jim. He's been summoned to the Prince. You'll treat him with the respect he deserves as a visiting dignitary, or you'll answer to me." I stared Anselem down, something I could do pretty much any time, with very little effort. He was older and a lot taller, but not a particularly strong individual, mentally.

He sniffed behind his hankie. "You think you're hot shit, missy, but we all know. We know what you are, now. I don't think you'll continue to be in the Prince's good graces much longer."

"Be that as it may," I said, voice low and almost snarling, "but at the moment I continue to hold that confidence. Now treat Jim here as an emissary, and let us in, or I swear to all that's holy I will beat your pale, poncy ass." I might be short, but when I got provoked, I tended to look like I got bigger. It intimidated some people, especially those like Anselem. He backed up half a step, his eyes looking for an escape.

"Fine. See if I care. Go on then." He pulled his clipboard up, pretending to be engrossed with checking things off. Anselem was sometimes okay, often over-officious, and today he was being downright irritating. I hissed at him, a warning sound, and he recoiled slightly.

Dez put a hand on my shoulder and redirected me down the hallway to the elevator.

"What the heck was that all about?" he asked as we got out of Anselem's hearing. "Are you trying to piss off everyone?"

I hustled along the corridor, smashing my thumb into the elevator call button. "He's a fussy old prick, Dez. My patience is non-existent right now."

Jim said nothing. He stayed silent and observed everything going on around him, following us as we made our way up to Magnus and his court. The long, maze-like path from the main elevator to the throne room was designed to confuse anyone unfamiliar with its turns. I kept a close eye on Jim as we moved along those hallways.

"Well, you need to get your patience and your temper under control, Alexandra," Dez finally said. "Otherwise, Magnus or someone will use it as an excuse to expunge you from the city. I don't want you to give them any excuses."

"Well, maybe they ought to think about how I'm feeling for a change," I retorted. "Things are fine between me and Magnus. The others will have to fall in line."

Dez shook his head. "It doesn't work that way. He has to continue to hold the confidence of the Elders of the city. He rules, yes, but technically at their behest. If they feel he isn't doing a good job, or is endangering the vampires within the Vancouver limits as set by council, then he will be removed and replaced."

I shook my head. "What the actual fuck, Dez? Who are our Elders then? Have I met them?"

"Some of them, yes. You've met Dario, Magnus' maker. He is one." Dez glanced over at Jim. "But that's a subject for another day."

I let the subject drop, despite being angry all over again. I gripped the packet of booklets to my chest, and marched forward at a reasonable pace for Jim. The doors were open when we reached the throne room, and we went right in. There were many people in the room tonight. Some were in the far corners of the cavernous room, and a handful clustered around the throne and Magnus.

I approached the dais on which the throne perched, and bowed deeply. I felt Dez do the same beside me, and Jim attempted to follow suit, though he was awkward.

"What do you have for us, Alexandra Immortuos?" Magnus intoned. I noted the title change. I was no longer "Alexandra of the Sanguinem" to him, or to them. I wondered how many of the flock of men and women were Elders.

"I have questions and requests, more than anything, my Prince." I opened the package, and brought out the books. A couple of the vampires nearby pulled back, as if distancing themselves from the presence of the literature. I rolled my eyes and snorted.

"Ask." Magnus was officious at times, and now was one of those times. He sat ramrod straight on his throne, looking like a statue. Clio hovered off to his left and behind him, a stack of things on a table that was out of his reach. The people nearby lounged on the steps of the dais, or on chairs, or simply stood. Everyone stared at me.

"These books are from the era of the other Immortuos. From the time of their eradication from the world," I stated, holding them up. "I don't know what they contain. I don't speak ancient Italian, and I'm hoping someone here will be able to translate for me."

A short, stocky man with broad shoulders and an olive complexion stepped forward. He couldn't have been more than an inch taller than myself, though he was much more broad in the chest. He would have looked like a mobster if he hadn't been wearing a knitted beanie cap and an Iron Maiden tee shirt with jeans. As it was, he looked like someone pulled out of time. "I am Pietro Soranzo, lately from Venice. I speak that language, and indeed, I knew the author of that series of booklets." His face was placid, pulled into a slight smile as he indicated the papers I held to my chest.

"Would you be willing to sit with me and go over some of the information in them?" I asked. "I cannot control what it is that I am. My blood has spoken; I am Immortuos. It's necessary for me to learn enough about my own history and that of my family. I want to avoid whatever mistakes and errors led to their destruction."

"Yes, and you will want to learn how to destroy the abomination behind you," he noted in a acid tone. He indicated Jim with a beefy hand. "That cannot be allowed to continue to wander the city."

I pursed my lips and closed my eyes. I counted to ten in three languages, then took a clearing breath. "I definitely need to learn the necessary spells to return Mr. Hale to his eternal rest. That is non-negotiable. I also need to learn about what I can, cannot, and should not do. Part of the reason we are in this mess is that no one anticipated the resurrection of a blood line long dead. Because of that, I wasn't taught not to do certain things. Experimentation is in my nature! I've helped our Prince on several occasions thanks to that nature. I expect to continue to be of service to my Prince and to Vancouver at large. I can only do that if I can use my powers efficiently and effectively. And I can't do that if everyone is denying I exist or threatening to kill me."

Pietro nodded in a thoughtful way, eyes half closed. "You are correct. Ending your existence would not solve anything. We would never know why your kind had resurfaced. Of course, there is always the possibility that you are not Immortuos as we knew them at that time. You could be a new variation of the Sanguinem blood line that also happens to be able to manipulate the dead. Regardless, you must learn to use your powers and not be used by them."

I hesitated a moment, and then said, "There may be more of my kind in existence, you know." I let it hang there for a moment, taking in the expressions on the faces around me. Some were bland about it, faces emotionless. Most looked scandalized by the thought that necromancers might be hiding among them. "I have a feeling that the line is not dead. In fact, it may have been carried forward by someone who escaped your pogrom. You were after abusers of their powers. If someone had escaped your scrutiny, flew under the radar so to speak, they could have continued the line. It's my hope that I will find others with more experience, so that I can learn. But that's for the future."

Magnus nodded. "Right now, our concern is with bringing about the rightful final death of Mr. Hale." I smiled at him, grateful to him for using Jim's name, and he nodded back almost imperceptibly. "And we must also deal with the entity that killed him in the first place. Clio, you had thoughts on that?"

"I do," she offered, stepping forward. "I have spent the last few hours researching. I've gone over everything about the woman seen in the photos and heard about from Mr. Hale and from Alexandra. I believe what we are dealing with is a siren. What I don't understand is why she is attacking random men at the waterfront."

"A siren?" I asked. "You mean a mermaid? I was right?" I looked over at Dez, triumphant.

"Not quite," Clio answered. "A siren is a specialized entity. She isn't an actual, physical thing, as we are, or Jim is. She is more spirit, and less aware of her surroundings. Normally they are called forward to avenge wrongs. But Jim here claims not to know the woman, and I believe he's telling the truth. Therefore, I can't understand why this woman is coming up from the waters to kill."

Pietro shook his head. "Sirens only happen in very particular circumstances. It's possible that they were first brought into existence in Venice, some centuries ago. I did some small amount of study of them, years ago. I can't see that your woman could be one. The conditions required are stringent."

Clio turned to Pietro. "I agree, it's very unusual. From what I have read, they are made of the ragged and unsettled spirits of horrendously abused women."

"Yes, but it is even more detailed than that. Sirens come about when, and only when, the woman dies of her abuse, and her body is dumped within a stand of water. Her body must then fully and wholly decompose there. It must remain undisturbed by sentient creatures until she becomes self aware. And even then, she only comes out of the water to avenge her own death." Pietro hooked his fingers into his belt.

We all turned to stare at Jim, who was standing there with a completely blank expression.

"Did you kill the woman?" I asked. I was horrified. Had I been harboring a murderer in my own home?

"No." He spoke with unusual vehemence, clasping his hands together in a nervous gesture. "I have never killed anyone!"

10 – The Truth Always Comes Out

"If he's a murderer, then he may be deceiving us," Magnus offered. "We have no way to know if he speaks the truth."

"Sure we do. Have Gabby or Clio or Dez compel him to speak the truth." I didn't include myself in the list, knowing I was too close to this issue to be trusted. I wasn't sure I trusted myself, to be quite honest.

"Summon Gabrielle. She's in the library, last I checked." Magnus pointed toward the room full of ancient tomes and scrolls, and one of his guards hustled out of the room. He returned with Gabby behind him. She looked at all of the stern and solemn vampires, and Jim beside me, and promptly poofed into thin air.

Dez sighed, one finger rubbing unconsciously at his temple. I couldn't help it, I giggled. Magnus looked cross, and Clio covered her face with her hands. Everyone else stood around, waiting, looking frustrated. Someone in the far corner of the room muttered about the fickle nature of the Impotentes.

I got myself under control, and whispered, "Gabby, it's okay. We need your help, please." We waited, some patiently and some not, until she felt she could return. It was an uncomfortable three minutes, but it's not possible to compel someone like Gabby to do anything. She had a tendency to vanish if she felt threatened. This was not conducive to a good working relationship. However, her talents were undeniably useful, and we required her expertise.

After a while, she appeared at my side, her hand snaking into mine. Her large, dark eyes were as big as plates. Once again, I was struck with the impression that Gabby was a young, innocent girl. This was incorrect, of course, but I wondered if it was just her nature, or if she used it as a kind of cloaking device. No matter how often you saw her hunt, kill, or stalk, you couldn't shake the visuals she presented. She was tiny, with a soft, round face, large eyes, a rakish mop of hair, and a thin build. She was a waif, and she dressed in a way that enhanced that image.

"Gabby hon, we need you to compel Mr. Hunt here. Jim needs to tell us the truth."

I will do it, but he has been telling you the truth, in his words. It's not the whole truth, but the words are true. She looked at me, solemn and mute, then let go of my hand and moved over to Jim. She took his hand in hers, shivering at the touch, and bowed her head. After a moment's concentration, she looked back at me and nodded for me to go on.

"Jim, did you kill the woman in the water?" I went straight to the subject. I didn't see any reason to beat around the bush.

"No, I have not killed anyone," Jim responded without hesitation.

"Do you know why the woman is coming after you?" I pressed.

"I… No, it's… " Jim's voice trailed off, and he fell silent. Gabby looked at me intently, waiting, still holding his hand.

"It's what, Jim?" Magnus' deep voice rumbled as he asked the question.

"I have not killed anyone," Jim repeated, and pulled his hand away from Gabby.

She returned to my side, taking my hand once more. He's telling the truth, as you know. But there's something he isn't saying. My powers are not strong enough to force the truth from him without you asking the right questions.

I sighed, and rubbed my temples. "At least there's that. But what are you not telling me?"

Likely he doesn't know for sure why she's after him, but the information he just got from you may have made him think about something. I can't compel him to say what he isn't sure about, though. Gabby shrugged at me. Then she bowed to the Prince, and returned to the darkened hallway beyond.

Jim watched the girl go, eyes restless. I watched him in return. I was uneasy, not knowing what conclusions he'd come to from our talking in front of him.

"Do any of you know of another Immortuos?" I asked, instead. "I somehow doubt I am the only aberration in the world."

There were murmurs and breathy comments, but no real responses. A couple of older vampires fanned themselves like the divas they likely were. But Pietro shifted, and the corners of his mouth twitched upward ever so slightly. I tried to convey my question in my eyes, and received a slight nod in reply. Whatever that meant. I hoped he knew something, and wasn't yanking my chain. I'd get my chance to talk with him in private later, when we were going over the booklets. I didn't have to rush that one.

Magnus cleared his throat, and everyone turned to face him. "Take Mr. Hunt down to the waterfront. See if your green lady has any interest in him. Use him as bait." His voice was harsh, uncompromising.

Dez looked over at me, to see if I was going to protest. I did not. I'll be honest, by this point I'd had enough subterfuge from pretty much everyone. I was ready to use anyone or anything as bait to move things along. If Jim would bring out this siren, then so be it. I didn't think she could kill him a second time, so it wasn't like I was risking his life.

"I will do as you ask, my Prince."

"I'd like to come along, if I may," Pietro interjected. "I am curious to see whether this green lady, as you call her, is indeed a siren."

Dez smiled to Pietro. "We would be pleased to have you, Master Soranzo. Your presence would be a pleasant addition to our company." He bowed, suddenly formal.

Four of us in the car. I guessed that Dez wasn't going to want Jim in the front seat. He also wasn't going to put a venerated guest and elder in the backseat, with a talking corpse that he'd earlier called an abomination. That meant I got to travel in the backseat. Of my own car. Damn it. This was not turning out to be a great weekend. I did a cursory bow in the general direction of the throne, and headed out, trying to tamp down my grumpiness.

When we reached my car, I opened the door for Pietro and let him get in. Dez gave me an apologetic look over the roof, which made me feel a tiny bit better. I decided to sit behind Dez, where I could reach around and touch him if I wanted. After Pietro was settled in, I held the door for Jim as well.

"I don't want to go." He stood there, not moving toward the car.

"Yeah, well, I don't want murderous green women killing people on my beach. I'm not getting what I want, either," I said, my tone full of all the venom and snark that I'd held back in court. "Now get in the car." I spat out the words, pointing my finger at the car.

"No." He didn't yell, and his tone of voice wasn't antagonistic, but it was also immovable, in the way a rock was immovable.

"Not an option, Jimmy m'boy. Get. In. The. Car." I spoke slowly, in a low tone, emphasizing each and every word. "Now!"

He didn't budge. Jim crossed his arms and planted his feet shoulder width apart. "I'm not bait."

"The Prince has said it, I agree, and yes you are. It's not like she can kill you." When he hesitated a moment longer, I grabbed his shoulders and pushed him bodily into the vehicle. He struggled for a moment, then stopped when his head almost connected with the top of the car door frame. He finally allowed himself to be seated and buckled in. I closed the door harder than was absolutely necessary, and huffed.

Dez stopped me for a hug before opening my door for me and handing me into the back of the car. I accepted gratefully, and eased myself into the seat, offering him a smile. He returned it, then got in the driver's seat, and we headed to Ambleside Beach.

❧

The beach was almost deserted by the time we got there. Dez parked the car in the spot closest to the dog beach, and we all got out. I had to strong arm Jim to get him moving, but at least he didn't need me to frog march him the rest of the way. He'd been silent and sullen the entire trip, staring at his hands, fidgeting. Now, he kept his eyes on the ground and his mouth shut.

"Where did you see her before?" Dez asked me, as Pietro joined us at the rock wall that provided safe puppy play space.

I pointed east along the trail. "There, where the bit of land juts out and the tree hangs over the trail. See, the light is broken."

"If she is a siren, her body has been dumped near here. Are there any quiet places that a woman's body could have been left undisturbed by human hand?" Pietro looked up and down the beach, seeing only the open waters.

"There are a few places. They're all east of where I saw her the other night. See the lit bridge? Past that, or around it." I nodded at the festive rainbow lights on the Lion's Gate Bridge beyond, an arc of color and moving tail lights. He nodded.

We found a bench hidden from the last of the humans who were making their way off the beach, and waited. I kept a hand on Jim's shoulder, standing behind him while he sat. I listened, searching for the sound I'd heard before. I waited, hoping for the annoying brain itch that would tell me she was near.

It didn't take long. Once the length of the trail was quiet, the last heartbeat fading into the city beyond the beach, I felt it. That burr against my brain pan had returned. I was about to say something when I felt Jim stiffen under my hand.

Dez caught the motion. "Do you see something?" he whispered under his breath.

Jim shook his head, and squeezed his eyes closed. "I hear it."

"I hear something too," I confirmed. "Or rather, I think I hear something, but I definitely feel something in my head." I gritted my teeth as it became more vivid.

Pietro and Dez scanned the area as Jim trembled under my grip. "Up you come," I said to him, and pulled him to his feet. "Head toward the spot I pointed out earlier." I nudged him in the direction of the jut of land and the tree. He moved, though reluctantly.

"I can hear her. She's… singing." He whispered, now, and his face was a rictus of fear.

"Do either of you hear singing?" I asked of the other two men. It had occurred to me that sirens might only work their magic on males. That matched the mythology, at least.

"Not I," Pietro said, and Dez also shook his head no.

"Dang." In seconds we'd crossed the short distance to the overhanging branches of the tree. The tide was lower tonight, and I shoved Jim with my hip, forcing him to the short wall of the path. I guided us over the lip of stone and onto the debris-strewn gravel beyond.

We made it three steps before Jim was twisting around in my grip and began fighting me to get off the beach. Whatever else was going on with him, his terror at that moment was quite genuine.

Dez moved ahead of us, closer to the water, while Pietro moved a short way up the thin ribbon of beach near the tide line. Both had their eyes on the rippling water. I kept Jim where he was, though I had to spare him a bit of attention to do it without harming him.

"Come out!" called Dez, and I felt a ripple of power from him that I hadn't noticed before. I contemplated that for a moment, until I caught a hint of movement in the corner of my eye.

Pietro backed away from the water, until the heels of his shoes touched the barrier wall. Unable to spare much attention, I forced Jim to the ground in a sitting position. He wasn't fighting anymore, though. He was gibbering, saying who knew what, his eyes rolling around unfocused and crazed. Whatever magic had held and summoned the man from the night before was not working on Jim tonight.

The woman came out of the water, a look of consternation on that inhuman face. She looked at each of us in turn, a slow and careful examination that seemed to penetrate to our souls. Then her gaze fell on Jim, and her confusion showed.

"Should not be here." She spoke haltingly, in a voice that sounded like water over smooth rocks. "He died. He paid. Why?" This last came out as a trailing utterance, ending as a moan of confusion and suppressed anger.

"Why did you kill this man?" Dez demanded.

Her dark eyes fastened onto his face. "Bad man. Awful things."

Below me, Jim groaned in abject terror, pressed against my legs like a toddler. His entire body was shaking. I braced myself, unsure of what I was preparing for, but trying to be ready nonetheless.

"What awful things?" Pietro inquired. I glanced at him, and he was standing braced to fight, but relaxed. Good, I didn't have to worry much about him. I didn't worry much about other vampires in general. Pietro had things to read to me later, though, so I couldn't let him be damaged. Still, he seemed capable enough, which made sense considering his age.

"The women, those girls, he hurt them," she answered in that sibilant voice.

"Jim, I think this would be a good time to fess up about whatever it is you figured out in the throne room," I commented. I stepped back away from him, and left him cowering alone on the sand. I had no idea what she would do. I just knew I didn't want to be too close to him if we lost control of the situation and she did it. "Got something to share with the rest of the class?"

He whimpered, hiding his face with his hands. "No, no, no, no," he babbled, and then mumbled something, incoherent with dread.

"Speak, now!" the siren demanded in a whisper. "Tell them. The girls."

I kind of wished we'd brought Gabby with us, so she could compel him into speaking again. His fear was rendering him speechless, and I wanted him to talk. I wanted to know what kind of monster we'd been harboring in our safe room. I had a feeling I was going to be horrified and disgusted by his response.

He sobbed, though no tears came. "I loved them!" he shrieked, the strident tone piercing the quiet we'd been preserving. I glanced around, assuring myself no one with a heartbeat was near enough to hear us. "I loved them, I did, all of them." He grabbed his head with his hands. "Make her stop, I can't stand it, make her stop singing!"

I sympathized to a certain extent, as my own skull's interior itched like crazy. I wasn't going to order her to do anything, though.

"What's your name?" I asked of our green lady.

She faced me, those misshapen eyes sorrowful. "Meredith Jones." Her answer came in a voice pierced through with foreboding. My heart broke for her, even though I knew nothing of her.

"What do you want with these men?" Dez indicated Jim, but the question included all of them. All of her victims.

"They hurt girls," she stated simply, as if that were enough. And it was enough, I supposed, even though it didn't answer the question in a useful way.

I nudged Jim with my toe. "Illuminate us. What did you do with these girls you 'loved'?"

"They agreed," Jim babbled, loud enough for us to hear him now, though not much more than a whisper. At least he wasn't shrieking anymore. "They said yes."

"How can a child say yes?" Meredith asked. It was the first full sentence she'd spoken, and her voice overflowed with anguish and pain.

"Not children. They weren't," Jim insisted. "They were 18. I checked. I checked every single time."

Geezus. My stomach was churning at the thought of some young woman being cornered by this man.

"Did they all hurt children?" Pietro asked.

Meredith shook her head no, seaweed rustling in her hair. "They hurt women. He hurt children. Girl children." She pointed a gaunt, elongated finger at Jim's cowering form.

"What did you do?" I asked again. Jim looked up at me with haunted eyes, pleading without words for something. "Tell us. In plain language." My tone of voice told him just how done with his shit I was.

"I courted them," he whispered. "I made love to them. I treated them so well, so well."

"You groomed them," Dez stated in a blunt, angry voice. The realization of what Jim had done was plain on his face.

"Yes," he whimpered. "And I led them on. And I took them places that were private. And then I had them. But they always left me," he added. "Always."

"I'll bet they did," I said, my voice acidic and outraged. "Once they figured out what kind of freak you were, I'm pretty sure they left you as quick as possible. Not quick enough, of course. I'll bet you scarred them for life, you cretin." I almost couldn't choke out the words, I was so furious. I'd had a friend in school who'd been raped by an uncle. It wasn't amusing, or minor, or acceptable. It was awful.

"He must die." Meredith still stood in the water, knee deep and completely unclothed. Her frail, bony form seemed strange and different, yet not out of place in the current situation.

I frowned. "He's already dead."

"He is not dead. He is here. And he must die." Her face was a moue of confusion.

"You killed him before. I raised him, not understanding."

"I will kill him."

Dez intervened, stepping to block Meredith's view of Jim. "I can't let you do that. I mean, leaving aside the concept that you can't kill him because you already did, I can't let you slaughter people. Humans. We can't allow it to go on."

"I don't know," I commented, and all three males whipped around to look at me. "He raped girls, and I'm not okay with that. I'm very not okay with that. Maybe we ought to let her tear him apart. Or whatever she's going to do." I crossed my arms over my chest, almost hugging myself, containing my anger and disgust the best I could.

"Hon, we can't do that. His soul is tied to his flesh because of your magic." Dez reached a hand out to me. I ignored it.

"Yeah. I know. And I get it. If we let her do this, he stays tied to the pieces she leaves behind, and continues to suffer. I don't see a downside to that." My eyes flashed, and Dez quirked an eyebrow then took a half-step away from me.

Pietro shifted position, keeping the siren in view but affording himself a line of sight with me as well. "That's quite morally ambiguous, Alexandra," he offered in a neutral voice. "I'm not sure what Magnus, as Prince, would think of that. You aren't the police, human or ours."

"Nope, I'm not. But it's obvious no one ever caught him when he was alive. She caught him, and now he's dead. Isn't that the right thing?"

"This is not something you want to do," Pietro cautioned. "It leads to a bad place, mentally. You said you were not like the Immortuos of 400 years ago, Alexandra. You need to prove that. You need to prove it to Magnus, but more importantly, you need to prove it to yourself."

I shook my head. "I am not like them. And I'll learn how to reverse things. But surely we can let him be punished." I stood there, an angry silhouette against the swirling water. I didn't want him to be allowed to escape this. I didn't want him to be released into the freedom of true death. I wanted him to suffer. He'd done things to others. He'd earned it. The revelation burned in me, a hateful fire licking at my chest, bubbling with anger.

Dez kept an eye on the siren, but approached me again. "Alexandra, you've made some passionate arguments about the existence of the soul. If you believe those arguments, then I implore you to take Jim and go. Find a way to return him to the death he deserved. Let me deal with Meredith."

My stomach churned. I looked from one to the other of them, and back to Jim. Meredith's face would haunt me for a very long time. The absolute truth of her statements was palpable.

"Not you," Meredith said suddenly, waving one ethereal hand in Pietro's direction. "I will talk to her. She understands."

I looked into her dark, hooded eyes and nodded. "Fine. Take him and go."

"Pietro, can you get Jim to the car for me?" Dez never took his eyes off me or Meredith. I could see the strain in the wrinkles by his eyes. His voice was calm, however, soft and even.

"As you wish, my friend." Pietro waded over to Jim, pulling him to his feet with ease. "Come along, Mr. Hunt. Time to go." They sloshed through the rising waters to the walking path, and headed toward the parking lot. I didn't spare them more than a glance.

"Alexandra, I'm going to go back to the path. I'm not leaving until you are ready to go. But I don't want to interfere. I trust you." Dez patted my arm, then retreated.

I felt the tears welling up in my eyes, and I brushed them away, angry and seething. "I can do this."

Meredith continued to stand in the water, which had risen up past her knees. Her body glimmered in a riot of color, in the lights reflected from the bridge behind her. I made my way over to her, and stood a couple of feet away, studying her. Her eyes flickered between Jim's retreating form, and me.

"He must die," she repeated, reaching out to me with both hands. "You know he must die." She shifted, restless and unable to find peace in the situation.

"I do know. He should have died, and I got in the way of that. I'm so sorry." Her hands met mine, feeling not quite solid, but not the mist of the previous night, either. "I will be taking care of that. It might be a little while, as I'm still learning. But I will reverse the spell and put him to rest. I promise."

"And me? Is there rest for me?" No tears flowed from those dark, cavernous eyes, but they glimmered.

"I don't know, Meredith. I hope so."

"I don't exist, not like I used to. Only sometimes. When I awake because one of them walks by. I can feel them. Their souls call to me. I can feel the wrongness in them."

"You can't rest because of what happened to you. If you can tell me what happened, maybe I can do something about it." I had no idea what I could do, but here was a dead person's shade or essence or whatever, and I was a necromancer, right? You'd think I could do something about it.

"There was a man."

Yeah, there always is, I thought to myself. "What did the man do?" I asked out loud.

"He hurt me. He hurt my sister." Her hands became less solid, and dropped through mine. I shuddered from the feeling.

"Was it a long time ago, or recently?"

She looked down, her fingers tracing in the water. "Not sure. The bay has frozen over twice since I first woke here."

I nodded. "So two years plus however long it took you to become aware. I will go do what I can, and I will come back soon. How can I talk to you?"

Her body sagged slightly, and she became misty at the edges. I reached for her, but my hand went through hers. "Call to me at the water's edge, near the big bridge. I will hear you, even if I do not come." And then her form began to drift apart, a mist over the top of the water. Her remnants were carried on the breeze, eddying around the lapping waves, until she was gone. I stood there alone for a very long time, as the tide came in and the water lapped indifferently around my hips.

It was the faint, far-off sound of a human heartbeat that brought me back to my senses. Someone was coming, and I needed to be looking a little more human and a lot less strange. I trudged out of the bay, pausing to wring out the bits of my clothing that were loose enough to allow me to do so. Dez watched me, but said nothing. His eyes were on the trail toward the bridge, where the heartbeat was moving closer.

Over at the car, Pietro had put Jim in the back seat again, and closed the door. He was calmly smoking a cigarette. He leaned against Jim's window, obstructing the view. I nodded to him, and he smiled back, though it was a little tight.

My heart was heavy, and I felt sluggish, and removed. It was like depression, but a physical thing rather than a mental one. Every step dragged. I kept looking back at the water. She'd dissipated like the unicorns into the waves in Peter S. Beagle's The Last Unicorn. "I will hear you," repeated in my head, like a broken record.

At that point, a man rounded the bend, talking into his cell phone, oblivious to the world around him. I felt the cramping pains of hunger hit me in a surge, and I tensed. All my instincts called out that he was prey. I was predator, and I could take him between breaths and no one would ever know. All my anger and frustration, my despair at being unable to make my magic work as I wanted, all the stress of the past few days boiled over. I was moving toward him at top speed, likely not even visible to him.

Dez hit me mid-stride, and I went off the path and into the gravel beyond it, now damp with the incoming tide. As we collided, he wrapped his arms around me tightly. We went into a roll that deposited us half way across the beach. The man didn't even look up. When he passed by the car, Pietro began singing a song loudly, sounding rather drunken. I geared up to fight against Dez, but he kissed me, hard. He bit me, and the taste of our mingled blood brought me back.

"We'll get you dinner in a few minutes. You need to calm down, Alex," he whispered fiercely, letting go of my body and holding my face in his hands. He brushed my bedraggled, salt stained hair away from my face, and kissed my forehead. "Calm. Let it go."

As he spoke, the dam inside me burst, and all the emotions I'd been burying came flooding out. I was silent, but I sobbed, my entire body wracked with them. He held me, rubbing my back until it passed. The salt water washed away the blood tears, leaving me empty, but feeling cleaner.

"We should take Jim back to the safe room and lock him up. Then we can eat." I took a deep breath, and steadied myself, inside and out. "I want to change out of these clothes, too. But at home."

"Let's go home, my love," he agreed, and stood, offering me a hand to pull me up. We meandered back to the car, where Pietro had ceased his singing after the man passed by.

"Everything alright then?" he inquired as we popped the trunk to pull out towels to lay on the seats. Pietro was largely dry, but Dez and I were still dripping.

"Mostly," I said, not meeting his eyes. "We're going back to our place. Can we offer you a ride?"

"Actually, I was going to ask if I might spend the day with you. I am ostensibly staying with Magnus, but he's a terrible bore. He made it quite clear that he needed some time with Clio." He grinned at me as he settled into the front passenger seat.

Dez held my door for me, then got into the driver's seat. "That's fine. You can stay in Alexandra's room. There's both bed and coffin there, depending on your personal tastes and needs."

"I try to avoid coffins unless necessary these days," Pietro chuckled. "I wouldn't want to put the young lady out of her own room, though."

"You won't. I sleep with Dez."

Jim stared sullenly out the window as we drove. It took every ounce of self control I had not to do or say anything to him. My anger bubbled beneath the surface, a frothy thing, threatening to explode. Home was not too far, but far enough, and I gripped my knees and focused on the back of Dez's head in front of me.

11 – The Scariest Thing Out There

At home, I stashed Jim back in the safe room while Dez got Pietro settled in my old room. I was walking out the door when Jim cleared his throat.

"Are you going to renew the spell?" he asked.

"I wasn't going to, no," I admitted, my voice cold and distant. "Why should I?"

"I don't want to go all stiff again. Please."

I contemplated the cretinous creature before me. "I don't really care about your wants, Jim. My raising you, that was not right, and for that I am sorry. But I have worked my ass off since the moment it happened, to figure out the correct way to fix this. In exchange for my hard work, you have lied to me, and deceived me."

"I know. I didn't know what to do. I still don't. But I can't go into rigor again. Please, for the love of God!" He started to walk toward me, but the warning look in my eyes held him back.

"I'll make you a deal. You tell me what you did, and how many times, and the names. You tell me that, and I'll consider renewing the spell to keep you out of rigor."

"I can't," he responded, shaking.

"Why not? I mean, it's your life. Or death, whatever. I don't care, quite frankly. That's my price."

"No, I mean… I literally can't. I can't tell you their names. I don't know all their names," he choked out.

I stared at this subhuman thing. "You knew you were doing wrong. That can't be denied at this point. If you thought you were in the right, you wouldn't have hidden it. You wouldn't have lied to me. You wouldn't make excuses. You disgust me. But fine, I will revise my price. You tell me how many times, what you did, and as many names as you can muster up. I'll even leave you a pencil and some paper, so you can write down any you remember during the day, as well. Take it or leave it."

I could hear movements beyond the heavy door. I knew that Pietro and Dez had finished upstairs and made their way to the family room. I doubted Jim could hear them. They were giving me my space, and might be listening in. I didn't much care. I flipped open my phone and turned on the camera, switched it to video, and began to record.

For the next forty-five minutes, Jim recounted the horrors he had inflicted upon his female victims. All in their late teens and early twenties, there had been about 25 of them. I sat there, silent, filming him. He remembered 14 names. Only 14 out of 25. I listened, my face frozen, my eyes dead, as he told me the details of those poor women.

He would befriend them on the internet. Age was such a tenuous thing there, and no one could know for certain how old or young someone else was. He would draw them in, get them to trust him. He'd ask to get together, always making sure to be 'safe' the first time by suggesting a public cafe or restaurant. He'd wine them and dine them, treating them as more mature than they were, lulling them into relaxing. And then he would finally, after a few dates, offer to drive them home. Instead of home, he'd take them down a back alley and sexually assault them.

When he started to repeat himself I stopped him. I fetched the blood, bespelled it, and fed it to him. "You are a sad excuse for a human. When a vampire tells you that, you know you're bad. But I will still work to complete this. I have done all I said I would, so far. I solved your murder. I have sustained you. And now I will work with all speed to dispatch you to whatever happy hunting ground you think you're going to. And may whatever gods you believe in have mercy on your soul… because I will not."

I left, locking the door behind me. Dez immediately jumped up and hugged me, then rubbed my shoulders and led me to the couch. One of Magnus' thralls was there, kneeling on the carpet by the coffee table. I remembered her from when Dez was badly wounded last year.

She smiled at me, and offered her neck to me. "The others have left. I waited for you. I heard what you did tonight. I wanted to be the one to offer myself to you."

"Why?" I sat down facing her, and Dez continued to massage me.

She tilted her head to one side, meeting my eyes with a serene look in her own. "I became a thrall because the vampires I met treated me better than my own kin. My father abused me. He hid it under a patina of respectability and righteous indignation. Magnus offered me a way to leave that. It's my hope one day to become one of you. You are helping a fellow victim, and you're taking care of an abuser. So I wanted to be the one." Her hands were folded in her lap, and she closed her eyes. She turned her head to the side and allowed her hair fall away to frame the pulsing carotid artery I could so clearly see and hear.

I couldn't speak, couldn't respond to her. But I took her, moving faster even than Dez. I moved her head into position, and drew her up to me. My fangs penetrated deep into her flesh, and I tasted the acrid flavor of the blood as it welled into my mouth. Dez hovered behind me, worried perhaps that I would try and drain the girl. He needn't have been concerned. I took what I needed, licked the wound so it closed without a scar, and released her.

"Thank you." I couldn't smile, but I nodded to her. Then I fled into the bathroom, saying nothing to either of the men. I drowned myself in hot water, scrubbing to remove a stain that had no physical existence. I heard Dez knock on the door a while later, but I'd locked it. Not that it would stop him if he wanted to come in. He could bust it open, or use the little emergency key that was stored above the door frame. The message was sent, though; I wanted to be alone.

The water had long gone stone cold when I finally shut it down, but I didn't care. I needed to hide inside the cloaking stream of water and allow the silence to be balm to my emotional wounds. It was near dawn when I finally made my way out of the bathroom. Pietro and Dez were still sitting on the couch, talking in quiet voices. They looked up as I came through.

"Come sit with us, love," Dez said, beckoning. "Pietro wants to talk to you about something."

I sighed, a tired and exhausted sigh, and padded over. I curled myself into the curve of Dez's arm. "Go ahead."

"I wanted to talk to you about your powers," Pietro began. "Magnus and the others believe you to be alone. I know this is not the case."

I blinked. Gabby had said as much, but here was confirmation. Pietro's tone of voice added a level of meaning to the statement, as well. "There are others?"

"There are. They are hidden, and solitary. They're afraid. Most are descended from the necromancers who hid from the pogroms of the 1600s. A few are like you, spontaneous spurs from the Sanguinem tribe."

"How do you know this?" I asked, and snaked my hand into Dez's, squeezing.

"Because I am one." Pietro sat there, leaning back in the big easy chair, looking very relaxed and chill. I felt my chest tighten with excitement.

"I thought he was one of us," Dez admitted. "He's always been introduced as a minor Sanguinem member. He's not terribly talented but he's older than dirt."

"The thing is, I am terribly talented. I'm just not talented at blood magic, because I'm not a member of the Sanguinem, as it were. But when I was made, the pogroms had already started. My lady, when she turned me, warned me to always hide within plain sight. A small fish in a big pond is rarely noticed."

"Can you teach me how to reverse my magic with Jim?" I demanded. "Can you teach me to control this stuff?"

"In time, yes. Though you already seem to have a good grasp of things. I am pretty sure you can figure out how to reverse it on your own, if you set your mind to it. But I will help you if you don't settle it by tomorrow." Pietro smiled at me, not unkindly, while I frowned.

"Why do I need to figure it out? I'm tired of reinventing the wheel." I couldn't keep the frustration out of my voice.

"Because you have a unique way of handling things and working your way through them, Alexandra. If I tell you, then you'll learn my answer. If you figure it out, you'll have your answer, and I can add my answer to the mix. Dez tells me you have quite the mind."

"I do, though not for sums. Please tell me that there isn't a lot of math involved with necromancy," I begged, trying desperately to keep from whining. Dez chuckled beside me. I poked him viciously, growling.

"Not much, no. Our magic tends to be more visceral, more empathetic. I sense that you know that already, though, based on the types of magic you've been doing. By the by, I'd like to learn the blood stone spell you've created. It has a delicious simplicity to it, and sounds incredibly useful. It would be good to know. We can teach one another," Pietro grinned.

"And now, I am taking my girl to bed," Dez said, firmly, rising, and pulling me to my feet. "It's been an exhausting night. Pietro, the light blocking shades in Alexandra's room are very good. You'll be undisturbed in there until she awakens and comes looking for her clothing. If you need anything, just ask."

～◈～

Dez's arms were holding me tight when I awoke the following night. He was awake already, but enjoying the closeness. I could tell because as soon as he felt me start to move, he licked my ear.

"Ew, Dez. You can be so gross." I pulled away, but he didn't let go.

"You don't get to call me gross anymore. You raised a dead person. You're a necromancer. Now we're both gross."

I wanted to be grumpy with him, but it's so difficult to be upset when someone is tickling you. I squealed, and kicked to get away, but he snatched my foot and dragged me back. This led to half an hour of noisy play fighting. Okay, it might not be as good as coffee, but it was a decent replacement.

When we finally made it upstairs, Pietro was sitting at the dining room table. He was sipping warmed blood from a coffee mug with a "World's Best Dad" logo on the side. I giggled a bit, and fetched myself a Doctor Who mug. I watched the blue police box disappear off one side and appear on the other via the magic of convection art, and warmed up my own breakfast.

"Right. The problem of Jim." I settled down at the table across from Pietro, plopping a three subject notebook on the placemat in front of me.

"Yes. That is, indeed, a problem. And as I said before, an abomination. Whether you succeed in making Magnus accept the Immortuos as a family or not, you must never do that again. There are many things we can do, both as vampires and as necromancers, that we should not do. But there are ways to get answers without animating corpses. Going forward, do not create abominations." Pietro spoke in a gentle tone, but it was also firm.

"I understand. If I'd known what would happen, I wouldn't have done it to begin with. I've been angry with myself for days now."

"Let's focus on the current problem. What is it, and how did you get here?"

I described the process I'd used to raise Jim. "When he actually began speaking, I about lost it. I was pretty upset."

Pietro laughed, an expression of wry amusement on his swarthy face. "I can imagine. What did you think had happened?"

"I thought someone else had made him into a vampire," I admitted, a little embarrassed. "I had never asked Dez how he made me, or how I could turn someone else, but I knew I'd been injured to near the point of death. I figured Jim hadn't started healing up yet."

Pietro nodded thoughtfully. "I can see how that would make sense."

"Anyhow, the basic premise is that I infused his own blood with energy that was meant to give me answers. I guess the magic decided that answers came best from a raised corpse. I need to learn to be more specific in my requests, so this kind of thing doesn't happen."

"That makes sense," he nodded.

"I'm glad it makes sense to someone," I muttered. "Well, once he was moving, I didn't know what to do. I kind of panicked. I brought him here, because I sure couldn't leave him there, all dead but animated on the side of the path. Since then, I have tried to use hair and nail clippings to de-animate him, but it hasn't worked. I thought it might be because I didn't have his own blood. The initial working was done with the blood that had been pooled around him. I assume that was his. But he has no blood now."

"Correct. So what is it you are actually trying to do, Alexandra?"

"I want him to die again. Or rather, become dead again. Return to his natural state," I clarified.

"Yes. And how is that related to the original working?"

I frowned. I didn't know the answer to that. How was Jim's second death related to my animating him? I thought it through. He had been dead, Real Dead. I'd used his blood to create a magical link between the place I could get answers (him), and the place that could vocalize the answers (his fresh corpse). So to reverse that, I needed to sever the link. But without his blood I couldn't do that.

But why couldn't I? Was the use of his blood incidental? Was my magic the common factor? I had to stop thinking like a blood mage and start thinking like a necromancer.

"It's hard to raise a family these days," I mumbled, low enough that I was not quite heard.

Pietro leaned forward, "What was that?"

"Well, unless they're buried close together," I finished, louder, my face breaking into a big grin. He started to protest, and then got the joke, and burst into laughter.

"Sorry, sarcastic humor helps me think," I finally said, after I caught my breath.

"You are quite the young lady," Pietro chuckled. "So what have you come up with?"

"I am thinking that the magic is what brought him back, not the blood I used," I started. "The blood might have been a contributing factor to slowing his decomposition rate, but I don't think it's the reason. I could have used whatever blood was around, and the magic as applied would have done similar."

Pietro nodded, listening intently.

"That means I don't need his blood in particular to reverse the spell. Since my original working was to find answers, and I now have those answers, I should be able to use any blood to fuel the spell to close it down. I should be able to..." I stopped, thinking. "No, that's not right." I sighed.

"Keep going," he urged. "Follow the thought."

"I was going to say I should be able to use blood to shut it down, but it doesn't make sense. Spells work, and then they're done. I did the spell, it animated him, and that was the end of it."

"Right." Pietro waved his hands. "And?"

"Oh, wait." A plus B equals C. Spell with focus equals result. The focus wasn't on answers, that was its purpose. The focus was Jim, because of his blood. But I could focus on Jim in other ways. So spell, with focus on Jim, should de-animate him. "If I use blood to do a spell with a purpose of separating his body and soul, that should do it."

"Ah, she discovers the KISS principle!" Pietro crowed. "Congratulations. I suspect that will work very well."

"Kiss? What's that?" I shuddered at the thought of locking lips with Jim.

"It's short for 'keep it simple, stupid'. When attempting magical workings, always go with the simplest version you can come up with. It's one of the problems I have with the Sanguinem. They seem to have an unholy aversion to simple things. They want all their math and symbols and Latin chanting. It's not necessary, in my opinion."

I held out my hands in a Hallelujah gesture. "Exactly! I've been saying that to Dez for EVER!" We grinned across the table at one another.

"So get yourself some blood. Let's see if this works."

I nodded, and went to the fridge and pulled out a bag. "Let's get it over with. It's either going to work or it isn't, and we might as well know now rather than later."

I headed out the patio doors and through the outside porch area. Pietro let out a low whistle.

"Nice digs you got, here," he commented. "I should come stay more often."

"You're welcome anytime, Pietro. And they are rather 'nice digs', I agree. I do think we need an inside stairwell to the safe room, though. I am tired of going out and in, or all the way to the other end of the house."

"You ought to install one of those pneumatic elevators," he suggested. "They don't take up any room, and they're fun. You can fit a coffin inside one, too."

"I don't want to know why that's relevant," I grinned. "But it's an idea. Might fit in the back area of the kitchen. I'll mention it to Dez."

We went down the outside stairs, under the porch, and into the living room through the double doors there. The safe room door was ajar, and I heard Dez inside. I could hear him calling me.

"Alex! I need you, now!"

I put on a burst of speed, sprinting into the room to find Dez kneeling beside a partially headless Jim. There was no blood, but it wasn't exactly pretty, either. "What happened?" I gasped out.

"Want… to… die…" Jim croaked out.

I closed my eyes and rubbed my temples. I was fascinated but horrified, all at the same time. He'd tried to end his life. Except his life belonged to me, because I had sealed his soul to his body. All he'd done is cut through some of the major muscles of the neck, and apparently his arms as well.

I knelt down beside Jim, so I could look into his eyes. "I told you I would sever your soul from your body. I do not make promises lightly, nor do I break them when it is in my power to keep them. You should have known this would do nothing."

"I had to try," he whispered. The callous part of my brain wondered how he was managing to talk. I could see that his windpipe had been severed. The vagaries of magic were many.

"I don't know if there's a God out there, or many, or if it's a void. But when I break the link, your body will expire, and your soul will go wherever it goes. You have blackened your soul, and I can't say that I wish you well. But you've suffered at my hands enough. This ends today."

I lowered myself to the ground, crossing my legs. I opened the bag of blood and poured a bit of it over my hands, smearing it over both. I closed my eyes, letting the inaudible hum of the blood enter me. I never knew how to describe that feeling to Dez; according to him, he didn't feel anything when doing magic. He just followed the formulae and it worked. Me, it was something I felt, something I manipulated, like putty almost, but not nearly so solid. I pulled that feeling up inside me, filling myself with its presence. I could feel the blood pulsing against my flesh everywhere it touched, almost a living thing on its own.

When I'd animated Jim, my focus had been both his own blood and the burning desire for answers. Now, I shifted my focus to completion, and endings. I visualized a silver cord connecting his soul to his body, a strong and pulsing thing. His soul appeared to me as a bright light made faint by tarnished and dirty glass, marred and flawed but still whole despite the filth. The cord ran from that light to a darkened husk, a dry and fragile thing that was crumbling and cracked. It appeared to be held together by an impossibly thin netting of wire coming out of the thicker cord. The blood in the bag and on my hands thrummed to the same beat as the light from Jim's soul. I reached out and dripped the glowing liquid over the center of his body.

In my mind's eye, the cord jumped as if it had been shocked, seeming to pull from the body. The thin tendrils that were entangled around the husk began to retract, and then let go entirely. I heard noises from Dez and Pietro, but ignored them, too involved in the vision of my mind's eye. The tendrils withdrew, becoming one again with the soul-light.

I had thought it would leave, then, but it hovered above the dissolving vision-body, bobbing lightly. I reached out my hand toward it, and it moved just out of reach, but didn't leave.

"You're free, Jim. But I see the tarnish on your soul." I spoke out loud, and felt Dez's hand go to my shoulder. I could sense Pietro shushing him, and staring at me.

The torture of living in my decaying body has taught me something, Alexandra, and I thank you for that. I know I am going somewhere now, and I will suffer, and learn, and then who knows. His voice sounded in my head, almost like Gabby's did, though not exactly. Death is not so bad. It's better than half-life. Farewell.

The light suddenly burst bright, and the container it seemed to be in exploded outward. I flinched, expecting to be hit by something, but there was nothing at all there. I opened my eyes. He was just gone, and his body lay on the cot, cooling and stiffening.

"It's done," I said, and slumped forward. The world wobbled around me, and everything contracted down to a tiny tunnel of light. I could hear Dez's voice calling my name, and then even that was gone.

12 – Tides Go Out, Too

When I came to, I was laying on our bed alone. Dez and Pietro were outside, talking in quiet tones but loud enough that I could hear them. A warmed bag of blood lay beside me on the table, and I sat up gingerly and helped myself.

They must have heard me moving, because the door opened all the way, and they entered. I smiled, feeling a little worn around the edges but otherwise alright.

"How are you doing?" Pietro asked, his eyes examining me carefully.

"I'm alright. Exhausted," I admitted. "He's gone."

They both nodded. "I know, hon. You did well," Dez said. "That was one hell of an explosion of magic, and I'm not surprised it took something out of you."

"Describe what happened," Pietro demanded, settling onto the end of the bed.

I went over the details of my vision. I described how I'd manipulated the energy and the blood, and severed the cord holding the soul to the body. Pietro nodded to himself as I spoke.

"And did you see the soul dissipate?" he asked.

I nodded. "I did, and I spoke with him before the blast. He thanked me." I frowned, unsure how I felt about that. I had spent more time liking Jim than hating him, but being thanked felt so wrong, and yet it was right, too. I was conflicted.

"Ah. And there it is." Pietro's face broke into a sunny smile, a strange thing on his usually solemn countenance. "The difference."

I looked confused. "What difference? I don't understand."

"Those of our clan who were exterminated 400 years ago were missing something. There is a… an ability to sense the pure soul of the dead, and not every Immortuos is capable of doing it. Most are. But for a long time in the late 1500s, that skill disappeared. When we can see the soul, the true soul, we can connect with it. A soul is not a person, nor is it a body. It is a separate thing. That ability to communicate with the soul allows us to see the good even in the worst of people. It's necessary, in order to avoid becoming callous and hateful. Many of our family line did not have it. They succumbed to the anger and bitterness that comes from working with the dead. The only way they could talk to the departed, was by animating the body. They forced the soul to speak through the leftover meat, as it were."

"But that's exactly what I did," I stammered.

"Yes, but you didn't do so on purpose. I needed to know if you could connect with the soul, though. If you could not, I would have suggested Magnus deal with you. You can speak with the soul; you don't need the meat to do the talking. The fact that you raised Jim's corpse was not a necessity but a mistake. Going forward, it's a mistake you need not make again."

I shook my head. "I'm sorry, Pietro, I'm confused. I don't understand. I don't have to animate corpses. I get that; no one has to do it. But isn't that what necromancers do?"

"In a word, no, my dear," he chuckled. "We communicate with and sometimes manipulate the dead, but that can mean souls as well as bodies. It's not recommended to raise a corpse unless there's some pressing need for the soul to have an anchor to this plane. That's the mistake our brethren made, way back when."

"Okay, so I can deal with souls. That's not a bad thing. Does that mean I can talk to the dead people in the morgue?"

"It's something to explore. I would say yes, though. You should also be able to tie a soul to this world, if it's necessary. You can release a tortured soul, a ghost if you will, provided it was not anchored here by another Immortuos. You can talk to the recently dead and ask questions, and sometimes guide them. Necromancers were also known as psychopomps at various times. They acted as midwives for the recently departed, showing the souls where to go and how to get there."

"So what about Meredith?" I asked, because she was the only tortured soul I could think of, at the moment. "Can I release her?" Dez hugged me, planting a kiss on my shoulder.

Pietro sighed. "I'm not sure," he said. "She is a soul bound to a physical form, but that binding was not made by a vampire, or even by a human. She was created and held to this world by obligation and abuse. Perhaps if we can put her bones to rest, we can then sever her tie and allow her to move on in peace."

"Pax et requiem," Dez murmured softly.

"Indeed," agreed Pietro.

ꙮ

A quick internet search on the Canada's Missing webpages yielded a photograph of Meredith Jones, and some basic information. Per her public file, she was in a known abusive relationship, and had last been seen some eight years ago. Her description was fairly close to the naked woman we'd met at the waterside. Of course she wasn't quite so gaunt in her picture, nor did she have the seaweed and such. Her eyes, though, were as haunted in the picture as they were in her ghostly face. That bothered me almost as much as the details of her death.

I took what I found and gave Clio a buzz. She got ahold of some friends in the police department. They forwarded private files detailing the investigation into Meredith's boyfriend, Jack Keefer. According to the authorities, Jack had a history of domestic abuse, past and present. They had been called to the Keefer home five times, but she'd never pressed charges. He was the primary suspect when she went missing, but with no body and no evidence of foul play, they had moved on. She was officially a missing person, not a homicide; their hands were tied.

Mr. Keefer lived in Edmonton at the moment. He was a skeevy kind of guy, with quite the rap sheet. So far, he hadn't been arrested on anything, but he was watched by both local police and the RCMP.

"Is it worth trying to get someone in Edmonton to do anything?" I asked.

"I don't think so," Clio replied. "It's a human. That's hardly a high priority for us. If it turns out that there's something that has a lasting impact on our society, we'll contact their Prince, of course."

"Alright. So the basic premise right now is that we need to find her bones, and from there, we can try and do a working to release her soul. That might stop the killings. Or might not. We don't know."

"Is Dez helping you with this?" she asked. I cursed myself for saying 'we', because Pietro wasn't known as a necromancer. Only I was. I didn't want to out him, even to Clio. Or especially not to Clio; she'd likely tell Magnus, and the proverbial shit would hit the vampiric fan.

"Yes, he and Pietro are helping. They're doing more blood and research stuff, and I'm doing more necro stuff." There, it wasn't an actual lie. It was a half truth. If I played my cards right, I'd open the door for Pietro to be honest about his inclusion in my family. I sighed, hating the dishonesty despite the necessity.

"It's okay, Alexandra," Clio soothed, misunderstanding my frustrated sound. "You can do this. I know you're not sure of your abilities, but trust in your instincts. I feel very strongly that you can do this, and that you're meant to do this."

"I know, Clio. Thanks."

Armed with the little extra information, I sought out Pietro and Dez, and brought them up to speed. They, in the meantime, had disposed of Jim's body in an appropriate, densely forested spot north of us.

"I want to find her bones. If I do, I might be able to use blood to sever the connection in much the same way we dispatched Jim's soul," I ventured. "I don't want to reinvent the wheel." Oh, how I was coming to hate that phrase.

Pietro frowned. "I'm not so sure about that. That was with a relatively fresh corpse that you were personally involved with raising. It's different when it's a body that's decomposed. I don't know that you'll be able to affect her that much. You'll also want to make sure you're well fed and prepared for this. It's going to sap you of everything."

"I figured, based on Jim's ritual. It's fine. I'll manage. We'll start fresh tomorrow evening, not tonight. I wouldn't trust myself to do it now. I was so shaky after Jim."

Dez kissed my head. "We will make sure you're well rested and energized for tomorrow."

"Pietro, it should be you doing this," I said. "I mean, you've been Immortuos your entire death."

"So have you," he quipped, grinning.

"Yeah, but my death is recent. Yours is definitely not."

"That is true. However, there's no denying you are the stronger worker." I started to protest but he held up one hand. "No, let me finish. First, you've done more in your few months as a fledgling than most vampires do in their entire un-lives. Second, you mastered some aspects of blood magic despite your clan affiliation. Thinking you were Sanguinem doesn't make you Sanguinem. Your ability to adapt rituals, learn, think outside the box, and reverse engineer is stunning in one so young. Third, and most important, you need to prove to yourself that you can do this. If I attempt it and fail, you'll never put yourself out there. If you attempt, you'll likely succeed, but if you don't, you have reason to keep trying."

I scratched at my nose, half smiling. I wished I had half the confidence these people had in me. I was pretty sure it was horridly misplaced confidence, but oh well.

"I'll try it, Pietro. I'm not afraid to try. I'm just not sure I can handle it. You have so much more experience."

"I have tons of experience at being a vampire hiding away in the shadows, pretending to be something I'm not. You have a lot of experience at being yourself. That's worth something, Alexandra."

I nodded to him, and pulled out my little notebook from my purse.

"Well, let's see. She said she was tied to a spot under the big bridge. I'm going to go with the basic idea that it's where her body is, or was at least. I should go down there and look for it."

"We can do that, yes. Being a vampire sometimes does come in handy." Dez grinned at me.

I was confused. "I don't understand."

"We don't need diving gear," he clarified.

I finally got it, and chuckled. "Very true. So if I do find her body, I will bring the bones or corpse up, and do the ritual on the beach. That seems to be the most sensible way to proceed."

"Why?" Pietro asked, curious.

"Well, if we're to lay her bones to rest, that's not going to happen in the water. We'll need to bury them. I'd rather not be doing that underwater in silt, breathing or no breathing."

"That makes sense. We should bring shovels, then."

"No, actually I have another idea…" I explained in detail to the two men, and the light of understanding spread across their faces.

∽ᴥᴥᴥ∽

The following evening, we gathered together and took our gear with us. We wore comfortable clothing that could get dirty, and headed to the Lion's Gate Bridge. We ate on the way, and brought extra in bags just in case. We parked the car at a small business across from the paintball place near the railway tracks, and made our way on foot to the area east of the bridge. We had to hop a couple of fences, but there wasn't any security to speak of.

We made our way to a small inlet, a kind of gravel beach of sorts which filled with water during high tide. Tonight it was swampy but not underwater, and we found a place inside the tree line. The sound of the cars above us was distracting, but not too bad. I stripped out of my clothing, retaining only a purple bathing suit I kept for midnight swim parties. I carried a large canvas sack and waded out into the bay.

Before I got deep enough for my head to go under the water, I whispered out Meredith's name. The muted call wafted across the water like the mist. I waited several minutes, trying to be patient. I took a deep breath, to provide me with some buoyancy, and started swimming.

Moments later, a tiny wake atop the water appeared beside me, and then her head broke the surface. Her dark eyes looked into mine, and I nodded, silent and solemn. We dove.

Far beneath the bridge, into the vasty darkness there, I found what was left of her. If I'd been searching on my own, I could have been there for days. Her form was bare bones, hidden and protected from the deep currents by a rock formation. Her bones, remarkably, were still pretty much intact. With as much reverence as I could muster, I placed each bone into the sack. I was shocked that some small pieces of flesh still adhered to the bone. The longer bones were more difficult, but I got them free. I may have missed some of the smaller pieces. I was hoping that "most" was good enough for the spellworking I was about to perform.

I was almost done when Meredith pointed to a single long bone, a leg bone, presumably hers. It was shackled to a large cinder block. This was what he'd weighed her down with. The sinew had kept her ankle fused to the femur. If not for that tiny bit of tissue, the whole skeleton would have drifted apart years ago. As it was, sheltered and held here, it had persevered. I struggled for a few moments, then managed to free it. It went into the sack with the other bones. I sifted through the sand for a few moments, reveling in the idea of being here, not breathing, just… being.

But Meredith was waiting, her dark eyes scrutinizing me. There was no judgment; only an enduring patience, like water wearing away a mountain. That sad look tore at my soul, though, and I pushed off the sandy bottom toward the surface so I could swim back to shore.

Did you know that vampires don't float naturally? I did earlier, because I had sucked air into my lungs. Balloons float, as it were. But then Meredith had led me under the water, and I had expelled that breath in order to dive. I had no other means of getting to the surface. Adding the nominal weight of the bones, there was not going to be a swim back.

However, upon thinking it through, I could walk. It would be a slog, but I didn't tire out from this kind of activity. I hefted the bag over my shoulder awkwardly, shifted by the underwater currents. I started trudging along the gravel bottom of the bay, toward the shore. It was interesting, that's for certain. Fish went by now and again, startled at the presence of this human going for a casual stroll at the bottom of the bay. My hair floated around me, and the water felt warm against my flesh.

When I finally broke through the surface, I could see Dez and Pietro standing on the beach. I waved, and they waved back. The going was quicker now that I wasn't fighting the currents and eddies. I made it to shore in very little time, and laid Meredith's bones on the stony shoreline. I arranged them with a tenderness and reverence that reverberated from my soul.

I started to talk, and water dribbled and spurted out of my mouth. That was another odd sensation. I must have taken a 'breath' while underwater, and had filled up. Not a problem for me, but it took a few moments to clear it all out.

"That was neat," I said, once I could get air through my vocal cords again. "And I was able to free most of Meredith's bones."

I looked out over the moon-stained surface of the bay, and saw her bobbing, semi-solid shape there. She would not come in, but could not leave. I hoped my plan worked.

"I need that blood now, Dez," I said. I held out my hand, and he deposited the vial of it into my waiting palm.

I settled myself down onto the bamboo mat that Pietro had placed on the beach, composing my mind for the work at hand. My eyes fluttered closed and I brought the vial of blood to my chest, cradling it there. I thought about Meredith. I pictured both the girl-woman from the pictures in her file, and the dark and terrifying siren hovering nearby. The sack containing her bones was by my right hand. I held the blood in my left, and my right reached down to loosen the neck of the bag and pull it open. As my hand brushed the smooth surface of the femur, my mental image of the siren sharpened. I visualized the details, filling in the mental image. She was neither young nor old, siren nor human, but all of those things at once.

The energy zinged as it pulsed through the blood in the vial. I exposed all the bones, as best I could, and pulled all that energy in a big circle. I let it roll through me, the bones, then the blood. It cycled, over and over again, until the three things seemed as one and the boundaries between them blurred. I panted with the effort of channeling it all, the speed of it making my head spin.

As the energy peaked, I pointed it all toward the bones. With all the will and mental effort I could raise, I spilled the blood over Meredith's remains. I visualized the silver cord locking her to her bones as breaking, shattering in a diamond shower of light and color. For a single still moment, everything hung in the air like a frozen image. Then the droplets fell to the ground around me in rainbow shimmers, and disappeared. All of it was gone, and I heard a final gasp, as Meredith's soul was freed from her earthly bonds.

My eyes were open, but I couldn't see anything. I could no longer hear the traffic above us, nor the water lapping against the beach. What I could see was Meredith standing on dry land, herself again. She was wearing the clothing she was described as disappearing in. Her eyes were no longer dark or sunken, and her cheeks were rosy and healthy. She had no heartbeat, and I knew this to be her shade, the last remains of her soul. She blew me a single kiss, smiling and glowing as if lit by a midday sunbeam, and then even that last piece of her was gone.

The darkness returned, normal night surrounding me. Above and behind us, the Lion's Gate Bridge shuddered as the many cars sped over its wide, modern surface. I collapsed on the mat, utterly spent. Things narrowed down to a fine, delicate point as I clung to consciousness. After a while, the tunnel expanded, and I came around. I lay on the bamboo mat, Dez hovering over me, Pietro still guarding the area with all his senses.

Dez helped me sit up, and when I motioned for it, he gave me a blood bag. Draining it helped me regain my composure somewhat.

"Hand me my towel and clothes. I'm done. I need to be dressed." Pietro looked away from the water reclamation plant to the north of us, and slid my bag closer. I dried off the rest of the way, and brushed away the sand and grit that was all over me. Dez picked seaweed out of my hair and relieved me of a snail that had been nestling in my hairline.

"You okay?" he asked, caressing my cheek. He examined me, his eyes searching my own before looking the rest of me over.

I nodded. "It's okay. It really is. She's free. It worked. And now we'll lay her to rest for her family, too."

❧❧

I arranged Meredith's skeletal remains beneath the beams of the massive bridge. We planted them in such a way that, in a day or three, the water would expose the weighted sack. The people who examine such things would know the bones had been moved, of course. There was no evidence pointing to us remaining on them, though. With luck, something in her remains might point to the man who had murdered her. Regardless, her loved ones would know she had not just up and left them. They would know she'd been murdered. It was enough.

Dez carried me back to the car, cradling me in his protective arms. Pietro cleaned up the scene of my ritual and then joined us. I was settled into the seats, buckled in, and Dez even tossed a blanket over me. This last was only for show, because I wasn't cold in the least and he knew it. There's a comfort in a familiar blanket, though. It held a faint hint of his cologne, and I nuzzled deep into it.

The drive home was quiet. Anticlimactic. The night seemed somehow brighter. I noted that the nights had begun to get longer again, and realized we were past mid-summer. Soon, there would be hours for enjoying life and love, music and movies and whatever else. For now, though, daylight came too quickly. Once home, we all went to our respective quarters and cared for ourselves.

I showered. The salt came off me, the seaweed, the bits of gravel that had gotten into the crannies it always does, no matter if you're human or vampire. I didn't feel dirty anymore. I felt light. I felt lightheaded, in fact, and so I was careful as I made my way from shower to bed. Dez waited, reading a book by the light of an oil lamp.

"Why don't you use the electric light?" I asked, towel drying my hair as I padded in, bare feet leaving little damp marks on the wood flooring.

"I like the color of the light from a flame better," he explained, smiling. "It's warmer. More human, I suppose. You're looking better."

"I feel better. Still exhausted, but not like earlier. I think I have a better grip on what I can do now. I think I have a better understanding of who I am. Of what I am." I sat down next to him, on his side of the bed. "I'm okay with being Immortuos. I can heal wounds no one else can."

"You most certainly can," he agreed. "And you can question the departed, get information no one else can. That can be helpful for Magnus and others in the city."

"I don't care about what they think," I said flippantly. "They can deal with what I am. I'm not going anywhere."

"There's my girl," Dez said, grinning. "You seem to have found your sassy pants again."

I clucked at him. "I am what I am. And what I am is a good citizen of the city of Vancouver. That's all I need to be."

"I let Clio know it was done, that Jim was gone and Meredith had been released. She said she'd let Magnus and the Elders know, and then asked us to come in tomorrow or the day after to talk to them all. I told her we'd be there when you felt ready to go, and not a moment sooner." He reached up and cupped my cheek fondly. "There's no rush, love. When you're ready."

I lay awake in the bed for a long time. I suspect that the faint strains of dawn were painting the sky before the day sleep finally took me.

13 – Necromancy For Fun And Profit

There seemed to be a distinct need for the vampiric aristocracy to tell me what to do. I'm not sure where it came from, but I was having none of it. I stood in the Prince's royal court room and stared him down. It should be noted that was no easy feat, as he was on a dais and was taller than me even when I was wearing heels.

"Alexandra, we can't have you just raising people. We can't. You must understand that." His lips were pressed into an angry thin line, and his arms were crossed over his chest.

"You're correct. I've learned some things about my vampire ancestors, no thanks to you and your murderous crusaders. One of the ethical traps they fell into was raising corpses rather than working on other levels. I have no intention of raising the dead again. This one time was accidental."

"And how do we know you won't have further 'accidents' in the future?" The voice came from the back corner of the crowd of Elders clustered near Magnus. I could hear the air quotes, and I resented them venomously.

"When I am aware of the rules, I stay well within them, sir," I spat. "That no one thought to inform me not to play with the blood of a dead man, that's on you lot. If it's that important, you ought to teach it to your progeny. You don't. None of you!" I waggled an angry finger at them, like a mother at her naughty children.

I paced back and forth at the foot of the Prince's dais, trying to contain my frustration. Dez was outside in the hallway, where I'd asked him to wait. I had to do this on my own. If I couldn't, then his intervention wasn't going to be of much help. Let's be honest, I was a big girl. None of that changed the fact that I wanted to smack them all, to a man.

The air quote speaker had blended back into his crowd. I couldn't pick him out of the crowd, of course. They did this on purpose, becoming a mob rather than a group of individuals. For vampires, they were depressingly human in their socio-political interactions.

"I have learned many things in the past few weeks. First and foremost, I learned that your pogroms do no good; bloodlines will always resurface at some point. You may quash the Immortuos line again, but there are others out there. Statistics tells us that quite clearly. It would not surprise me to discover there were other Immortuos hiding among you. After all, you've given them no reason to be open about themselves."

I met the eyes of each Elder, holding them until they were forced to look away. Pietro was the only one with a twinkle in his eyes, but he hid it well and pretended to shift in discomfort like the rest.

"You've gotten yourselves so hidebound that you can't see what's in front of your faces. Really, now! Most of you have known me for well over a year at this point. I've been an asset to this community, and I intend to continue being one. It gives me great pleasure to aid in the functioning of our society. I have a great love of what and who I am today. And part of what I am is Immortuos, whether you like it or not."

"You are not what the Immortuos of old were, though," Magnus pointed out. "You learned how to be Sanguinem first, and only later discovered your true heritage. It may be that it makes a difference." He glanced at his council, then back to me. "You aren't a bad person, Alexandra, and you're a good citizen. We know that. But enough of us remember the horrors of the necromancers in Italy and England. We have no interest in going back to that."

"Right. I understand not wanting to go back to the days of being ruled by superstition and blind religious fervor. That would be horrid." I let the sarcasm drip from my voice. "So instead, let's look at what happened back then, and figure out how it went wrong. Then let's make a point of not doing that."

I paused a moment, then continued, my voice calm but loud. "When I say that, I mean all of us. I want to be clear that nothing in the world happens in a vacuum. I don't know what happened back then, and I doubt any of you do, either. By destroying the written history of the Immortuous, you have made it nigh on impossible to find out what was going on among the other vampires. We have no idea what motivated the Immortuous themselves, to push them to act as they did. You are responsible for a part of what happened, and for handling it as poorly as you did."

Magnus nodded, and a few of the other Elders did, too. Not enough, though. None of them looked as uncomfortable or guilty as I had hoped.

"I have some of the histories of the time, from other families. I'm going through them with Pietro's help. I will learn what I can from there. But more than anything, I want to make our world a place where people can be who they are. I am a necromancer; you all need to deal with that. Killing them 400 years ago didn't work, and killing me now won't work. Instead, let's put our heads together and grow as a community."

"What assurance do we have that you won't go on some kind of spree?" Another anonymous voice expressed concern, while the milling vampires muttered agreement.

"None," I said bluntly. "I could go shopping at any moment, and clean out the Sanguinem bank accounts like that." I snapped my fingers. I heard a far-off snort of laughter, and guessed that Dez was listening in from the hallway.

More seriously, I continued. "There's never a guarantee for anyone's actions, gentlemen, ladies. You have to make educated guesses. I haven't done bad things thus far, and have no intention of doing them going forward. You've heard the details of what happened with Jim Hunt, and how it was dealt with. Pietro and Dez and others can assure you that my mistake was just that, a mistake. In the process of fixing that mistake, I made discoveries about my own skills and powers. There's no reason here on out for animating corpses; it's not good for anyone involved. I have no need, in any case, because I can connect directly with the soul of those who have passed on."

"But you maintain the ability to tie a soul to a rotting body!" A very young looking man in the front of the pack spoke. "How do we trust that?"

"In the same way you trust anything else. For heaven's sake, you'd think no one ever did anything shady in this city. My own death and subsequent vampiric awakening was in the questionable zone. The affairs of last year, when one of your own elders turned out to be rather insane and abusive, also comes to mind. You're hardly some paragons of virtue. Let's not forget that any one of you maintain the ability to go on a murderous rampage at any moment."

Magnus held up his hand as angry murmurs rose and began to drown out normal talking voices. "Enough! Alexandra, will you give me your word that you will not raise a corpse again?" His eyes held mine, a firm gaze, demanding from me a promise.

"I promise that I will not raise a corpse unless you or the Elders of this city require it of me. I can think of several cases where it would be useful for us, and so I refuse to make a promise that might not be kept. But I will bow to your communal wisdom in regards to who and when."

Magnus looked from me to the milling mob of city Elders, then back again. "Any dissents? Or can we finally move on from this?"

Pietro raised a hand, and stepped forward. I watched him warily. He'd been very pointed in asking me to maintain his secret, and I had done so. What was he up to?

"I move that the Immortuos be officially reinstated as a family within our society," he said. "I further move that Alexandra be made acting head of that family. She should work with Hades, that she might learn the knowledge required of a family head."

"Seconded!" Clio's voice rang out loud and clear. I smiled to her, and she returned it.

"Are we all agreed, then?" Magnus scanned the vampires present, and hearing no naysayers, continued. "Then as of today, the Immortuos are reinstated. However, as Prince of Vancouver, I want regular reports. I do not want the horrors of the past to be revisited. Therefore, you will work with Dez, and report to me at least once a week. Is that clear?"

"I have no problems with that at all, my Prince," I agreed. "If that is all? I'd like to head back to my home and start sorting through the buckets of paperwork this is likely to generate."

"We are not quite done," Pietro interjected. He faced his fellow Elders. "You've all known me for some time. I've been a well thought of Elder of Vancouver for some ten years, and before that, I was an Elder in Italy. I'm respected, and my research capabilities are second to none. What you do not know is that I, myself, am Immortuos. I knew even back then, during the culling of the necromancers. My maker, who was Sanguinem, wisely suggested I hide my nature. And I have. Until now."

Pietro walked over to me amidst gasps and titters, and lowered to one knee. "My lady, you are a capable and intelligent woman. You have been an incredible advocate for many different people in the last few days. I am beyond impressed. And I am here to pledge myself to the Immortuos and to yourself as head of our household."

"Oh, do stand up, Pietro," I chided. "Stand up, you silly man. Yes, I accept you. I suppose all that business about keeping things quiet is no longer required?"

He grinned. "I think that cat is out of the bag."

We spent the next hour explaining his part in our merry adventures. Magnus sighed, hearing about Pietro's duplicity over the years. There was no changing it, though, and that was that.

"I am going to censure you over this, Pietro," Magnus stated. "I appreciate your help in this entire situation, but I am quite done with lies and deception in my court and my city." He looked out over all the vampires gathered in the dark recesses of the room. "Make note of that. Each and every one of you! There will be no more trickery, no more hypocrisy, no more treasonous activities in this city. Trouble may come of telling the truth, yes. From this moment forward, beginning with Pietro, the trouble generated by outright lies and untruths will be greater. Far greater!"

Pietro bowed his head, a humble gesture, and moved to the base of the dais. "I will accept whatever punitive actions you consider necessary, my Prince. I do not pretend to have been truthful with you over the past decade that I have lived within your borders. I will state for the record, however, that my family affiliation and skills are all that I've misled you about."

"And that is what will save you, my old friend," Magnus replied. "I hereby demote you. You are no longer an Elder of this city, or any other. You are just another citizen of the city of Vancouver, and you will work under the head of your household. As you've declared you are Immortuous, that means you now belong to Alexandra."

I started to protest. "I can hardly say I own him, Magnus!"

"Enough!" Magnus barked, cutting me off. "For the next twelve months, Pietro will be nothing more than your lackey, your assistant. That is his punishment. It's lax enough."

Pietro bowed his head, and moved over to stand by me. I grumbled under my breath, but stopped after Magnus shot a dirty look at me.

Then he turned to the throng. "Do not think you can do things in this city that are contrary to the rules we have agreed upon. If you don't like our rules, you can leave; no one is forcing you to stay. If you stay, you will follow the rules. This is not a suggestion, it is a requirement. It applies to the youngsters who wander the back alleys at the dock. It also applies to the Elders who work with me to run Vancouver. It applies to me. Do you understand?"

There was a dead silence for a long moment. All movement stopped, and all eyes were on Magnus. Though he wasn't tall, he could be very regal, and this was one of those moments. As the room took a collective (unnecessary) breath, heads began to nod in agreement. The tension in Magnus' shoulders released, just a touch.

"Now go away. All of you!" Magnus waved his hands at everyone, dismissing the entire group in one gesture.

"Get off my lawn, you damn kids," muttered Pietro under his breath, and I giggled. The strangled look in Magnus' eyes caused me to high tail it out of the court and the building at high speed. Pietro, Dez, and everyone who wasn't as fast as me followed behind.

❦❦

As we entered our home, Dez looked about, his gaze critical. "You're going to need your own space," he commented.

"Um, no!" I said, offended. "You aren't getting rid of me that easily."

"I don't mean you moving out, hon. I mean you're going to need a proper office, and we may need more safe space room, depending. If new members of your family start coming out, there might be need of them to stay with us."

"Oh." That made sense. I was going to be responsible for caring for and checking on all the Immortuos, if they exposed themselves. Our little safe room could only hold one or two in any comfort. We would need more room, indeed. "What did you have in mind?"

"I think we should buy the house up the road. It's not quite as big as this one, but would make an excellent second property. It has a bit of land attached, and the acreage between our two properties could house an underground bunker, over that way." He pointed along our tree line, as we moved out onto the patio and looked east. "If we have our own contractors do it, it will be hidden from the humans. We'll build a bunk room, and an emergency bolt hole. We can attach it to both houses via underground tunnels. We'll include an extra exit to escape through, should it ever be necessary."

"That sounds expensive." I looked over the forest between the houses with a critical eye. "But it could be done."

"We can move our living space into the second house, all designed to be private and just for us. Then we can turn this house into offices and safe space. That way, we have room to get away from one another once in a while, but we can still work and live together. And there will be plenty of room for the inevitable filing cabinets."

"I could do much of our filing paperless," I suggested, teasing him.

"And risk losing it because of a power surge or outage? No thank you. Paperless is fine for some things, but hard copies must be kept. I'll show you. It isn't rocket science. It isn't math either, by the way," he grinned, poking me in the side.

"Jerk," I said, smiling. "I like the idea. Is the property next door even for sale?"

"It is. I had noted the sign went up last week, but it seems to be timely. I'm sure you'll like it. It's a bit more cozy, and there's a wood stove instead of a big fireplace like this one. But we could be happy there."

"I'm happy so long as we're together, Dez. I mean it."

"I couldn't agree more." He planted a kiss on my forehead, and led me down to our room.

His tenderness was always a balm to me. All my hurts, internal and external, were healed when I was in his arms. Even his gentle touches were tempered, however, with that little touch of strength. That little hint of the predator never went away. It made me happy, knowing that we could always be exactly what we were with each other. We didn't have to hide anything away. It was right. It was as it should be.

❧❦

There was so much work to do! I had to pack up our personal things from the old house to move them to the new one, and even with Dez's minions it was a time sink. Then there was paperwork about and practice at necromancy, which was exciting but also scary and emotional. I also had to make certain that I showed up to court on a regular basis with reports on what I'd done, and when, and with whom. I was dizzy, stressed, and felt distinctly frayed at the edges.

Pietro helped, and turned out to be an incredible archivist. I was overjoyed, because keeping notes on random activities just seemed boring to me. Pietro, on the other hand, reveled in it. As each new Immortuous arrived, he would take down their information and note their general skills and powers.

"This is the history of the future, Alexandra," he explained, happily stacking piles of notes. "Done right, these papers will be looked at in a hundred or two hundred years, and the re-acceptance of the Immortuous will be a glorious piece of trivia. It's important they be kept organized. Your successor may need to reference these, or the head of some new family!"

I chuckled wryly. "Pietro, I believe you're the only person who gets this excited over administrata. But I'm glad you're on board, because I definitely do not like that aspect of this job."

"You take care of the teaching, and I'll deal with the filing. We're good, Alexandra."

I shook my head. "Why am I teaching instead of you?" I was preparing the lessons for the following day's meeting of the Immortuos.

"First, because you are the head of the household. They expect you to be teaching them. It's your job. Second, because by teaching something, you learn it better yourself. If you're helping others learn, you're cementing those lessons in your own mind. And third, because I hate working with people in general, and won't do it. You, I don't mind teaching. Them? Not on your life." He grinned, and handed me a stack of papers, copies of the latest translation he'd done of some papers from Venice.

"All good reasons. I still wish it was you teaching them." I sighed, and slid the papers into my briefcase. "At least these lessons are ones I excel at. I got very tired and angry over not being able to learn the stuff Dez was teaching me. I sucked at it."

"Well, that's understandable. He thought he was teaching you something simple, something any first year Sanguinem should be able to master. And he was correct that any new member of his house should be able to do it. You're just not in that category. I'll be frank, it's amazing that you can do the amount you do. You're almost a hybrid, between Sanguinem and Immortuos."

"How so?" I frowned. I didn't like it when things didn't fit into neat pigeonholes. I wanted everything to be organized. Clean. Focused. Having navigated the minefield of getting the Immortuous back into the world, I didn't want yet another hurdle to jump.

"You did manage to master some of the easier spells the blood mages use. That's unusual. As you know, those talents run within families. It's a testament to your temperament. You are catching onto the basics of necromancy with extreme ease, as well. Perhaps you're neither blood mage nor necromancer, but more… death mage. Or soul mage," he offered.

"Soul mage. I like that." I flipped open my phone's translator and looked it up in Latin. "Animamortum," I said. "I'll keep that in mind for myself."

Pietro chuckled. "Nice. Never let someone paint you into a corner."

"No one puts Baby in the corner," I quipped, smiling. "Anyhow, I guess we're learning how to connect with the spirits of the long dead this week." I patted the bulging briefcase. "I thought we'd take a walk down to the Boal Memorial Gardens. A lot of people go there to walk in the woods and be quiet and meditative. I've picked tomorrow because Thursdays are rarely busy."

"How many of you are there?"

"Only six, including myself. We'll all wander in and go to the reflecting pond. There are always a few souls hanging around. We won't bother anyone, and we can focus on hearing what they have to say."

"It sounds good. But why not a bigger cemetery? Surely there would be more souls around to talk with." He tilted his head, examining me.

"A bigger cemetery also has fresh souls, and some of them are turbulent. And some are very much still connected to their corpses. I don't want to risk teaching bad habits. Boal only has urns; they don't bury bodies. The connection is broken long before we arrive. Any souls are there because loved ones visit them and talk to them, not because of their bodies. Zero danger that someone will create a zombie, and that's a good thing."

Pietro nodded. "That is good. You don't want to be setting people up to be traumatized. Enough of your students are traumatized just being certain of what they are. They often want to remain bad Sanguinem rather than good Immortuos. It's a tough row to hoe."

"I know." I blew out a long breath, making a raspberry with my lips. "But they have to learn. If they don't, then they could make a mistake, and then I and the whole family get in trouble. We're not going there again!"

I packed up the last of what I'd been working on and closed up the briefcase. It was dangerously distended, and I eyed it as if it were a bomb about to explode. The analogy was more apt than you might think, considering its contents.

14 – The Necromancer's Club

Creating a vampire family out of whole cloth was not easy. The clans and families currently in existence had been around for decades, if not centuries; their founding documents were lost to the dusts of time. I couldn't look at old Immortuos files because they had been burned along with their authors. I was stuck reinventing the wheel, as it were. It was tiring. It was frustrating. Sometimes, I wanted to bash my head against a wall.

And then there was the rest of the time. With the public and official acceptance of the Immortuos family, Magnus had opened the door. A handful of locals came to visit me, vampires who had ostensibly been blood mages as far as anyone was concerned. Apparently, a number of the 'lesser talented' Sanguinem were actually Immortuos. None of them had any clue as to how to use their powers.

The ones who knew, though, were easy to deal with. They wanted to learn. It was the ones who had never fit in, who had no idea why their supposed powers didn't work, who were difficult beyond belief. Not all of them were Immortuous, and I hated not being able to help them.

We had visitors from other cities and parts of the world, coming to sign in as members of the new family. It was fascinating as often as it was irritating. I found myself drowning in mail from around the country, and had to bring in others to help me process everything. Magnus, too, was overwhelmed with messages from the Princes in other places, asking what the hell was going on. He dealt with his own correspondence by explaining that he wasn't one to buck evolution. He let them know that if they wanted more questions answered, they should talk to me. Gee, thanks. Not.

I went from being a lone necromancer, to being one of many. There was myself, Pietro, and two other previous members of the Sanguinem, all from the Vancouver area. Dozens of others contacted me as well, asking about training, and organization, and what was allowed.

I don't know what I'd have done without Pietro, to be quite honest. I accepted his offer of help with extreme gratitude . He not only spent countless hours going through paperwork and letters, he translated old Venetian texts into English. He also began teaching me. I, in turn, taught others.

I also spent some time figuring out what the basics were of necromancy. There had to be a way of testing for this. Yes, progeny of known Immortuous were almost always also Immortuous. Almost, but not always, because life (and death) are complicated. How did you test to see if random vampires were members, though?

I tried to find simple things that came easy to me, that I could use as identifiers for future applicants.

Seeing "ghosts" was a simple test, for example. I had only known Immortuous to be able to see them, so far at least. If I could be in a room with a ghost, and my applicant could see and interact with them, we were golden. But not all Immortuous have that particular ability without training. A success meant you were in, but a failure did not mean you were out. And ghosts weren't exactly common; you had to go looking for them. They generally didn't hang out in my office. It was, as with all things vampire, very convoluted.

&&

In the weeks since I'd dispatched Jim and released Meredith, so much had happened. Dez had purchased the property next door through his land agent, and we'd begun the process of connecting the two homes via tunnel. It was being done deep into the tree line, where most people wouldn't see much of what was going on. The plan was to muddle memories of the humans who did the work, after it was complete. We wanted to ensure that our sanctuary very private.

Dez was covering his underground digging at night by having work done during the day on the new place, to make it more vamp friendly. The day digging required the same equipment as at night, for slightly different purposes. Currently, they were putting in two 'disappearing' parts to our new home.

The first was an underground parking garage, which would eventually connect to our underground tunnel. The parking pad for it came up into the Sanguinem House driveway. You drove your vehicle onto it, and then it descended into the ground. It ran on solar power backed up by grid electricity. I thought it was hysterical that vampires were harnessing sun power from their coffins. It appealed to my inner sense of snark.

It was all insanely expensive and stupidly intricate. I'm sure it cost more than what I made in three years as a secretary. But man, it was so awesome! It also meant that any cars would always be out of sight, thereby never alerting the neighbors to how many people might come and go from our place. This was important because of the new people arriving almost daily (nightly?) to talk to me. The underground space allowed for comfortable parking of up to twelve cars. We discovered that, with practice, we could squeeze fifteen in. It meant a lot of car jockeying, though.

The second disappearing item was my pool. It was a marvel of modern engineering. The backyard of the new place wasn't as sumptuous and spacious as our original one, but did have a very flat, open piece of ground. Dez wanted to have a pool put in. I wanted a patio, though, because I had come to enjoy sitting in the dark, watching the stars at night. There was a peacefulness to it. Not having enough cleared space, he did the next best thing: he had my patio designed to go down into the ground, exposing the pool underneath. It required a bit of sweeping before you let the teak decking go down into the water, but it was a pretty maintenance free pool, otherwise. Not that it mattered. We had a pool boy, and minions.

The new house was smaller than Sanguinem House, but had three levels along one side. The master bedroom was in the basement, and sported a huge sunken window. We had that covered, of course. All the windows and doors had enclosed blinds installed, designed to block all light from entering. As for decorating, he handed me the checkbook.

Note to future lovers: never hand me the checkbook. I had fun.

The best thing about the new house, though, was the library. It wasn't huge, but it was its own spot, off the living room. There were three walls of built in floor-to-ceiling bookcases in dark mahogany. I ordered a fat, overstuffed brown leather chair and a side table that raised and lowered. This was my private work space now, where I could go to be quiet, research, or relax. I also ordered a ridiculous number of books for the library. Having a library meant I had to have lots and lots of books. Sexy, I know.

Far beneath the ground between the houses, below the trees and bushes and animals, we were having a bomb shelter put in. We'd thought about various ways of making an underground living space, but bomb shelters were cheap in comparison to custom builds. You could also order them pretty anonymously. It was an L-shaped affair, with two bunk rooms. It also had a composting toilet (for humans that came along for the ride, I suppose, as we didn't use it), and a galley kitchen. It even had a periscope. You know, for looking up into the forest to see if the coast is clear... or the nuclear fire has died down. Whatever.

It was a lot of expenditure, and we didn't care. Money doesn't mean as much when you've had a savings account for almost a hundred years, and you don't eat food. Or care if the heat is on. Or the lights. The coffers were full, unharmed by mercurial human politicking or economy. What we built was meant to last, and last it would.

Sanguinem House became Mageholme, and it housed a variety of blood mages and necromancers as needed. The new place became our own private home. Mageholme was a hub of activity most of the time, with much of it taken up in public meeting spaces. This, in turn, relieved a lot of the pressure that had been on the Annacis Island court and Magnus. The public parts of his library were moved to the house. The downstairs rumpus room into a full on library that was three times the size of the one Magnus had kept. Magnus even held court at the house sometimes, which was nice for us, as it meant we didn't have to go out.

With Pietro's help, I learned more about my own powers. I had no problem talking to the recently dead. I could often see energies or spirits, sometimes from those trapped in our plane and sometimes those who were out for a wander. I could still revive a corpse if needed, but I couldn't think of a reason why I'd need to do it. With practice, I found I could conjure a soul to speak to me, without ever touching the body. This was much easier on both the soul and myself.

I also discovered that souls were much like people, at times. Newly dispatched souls were often confused and unsure of what they were doing. I could guide them to look for whatever it was that took them to… the other place. Those souls often shone like candles, whether they had been good or evil in life. The souls of those long dead, those who hung around to achieve goals or watch over their progeny, were as varied and different as their living counterparts. Some were nice, others were assholes, and there was a wide spectrum in between. I dealt with them with the same patience, loving-kindness, and snarky attitude as I dealt with the living. Everything was going well.

There were definitely moments, of course. I had a run-in with an angry and rather ghostly gentleman that spent a surly hour demanding he be issued a harp and white robe. I wasn't sure what to say. Maybe that part happens after you get to heaven, and he was still destined to head that way. Maybe he had been denied heaven. Maybe there was no heaven at all. There was no way for me, the poor necromancer, to know the answer to all that.

Of course, the same went for all the other religions. Wiccans were looking for their Goddess. Buddhists looked for Buddha. I even met one lady who was waiting to see if the Flying Spaghetti Monster was real, I kid you not. I could not make this stuff up if I tried.

Talking to ghosts was easy. Often, they could make themselves visible to me without me even trying, appearing as I walked into a place where they were standing. Usually, I needed to be concentrating at least a little to see what was floating around wherever I was. Most of the time they were happy that someone could actually talk to them. They would make conversation for as long as they could. If I was lucky, I'd hit on whatever it was that was bothering them. They'd suddenly realize their personal quest was complete, and that lovely flare would happen. They'd say goodbye, then poof. That always felt good.

The hardest part was probably when a family was grieving and their dearly departed was grieving on the other side of a veil they didn't even realize was there. You can't go over to a sobbing widow or adult child and say, "Hey, grandma is fine even though she's dead. If you stop crying and tell her you love her, you can all move on!" It doesn't work that way. I know, because I tried that a few times. I spent a lot of time, those early months, looking at kittens on the internet as a coping technique for my stress.

On the other hand, dealing with little kids was pretty cool. I didn't often get to see them, only being around in the dead of the night as it were. The few times, they had strayed away from late evening funerals and I could talk alone to them. Little ones, kids up to about age eight or so, seemed to deal just fine with a weird, dark lady telling them that mommy or daddy says they love them, and all is well, and to be good for Aunt Martha. Kids are resilient. They also haven't been taught everything that isn't supposed to exist. After all, they know monsters exist, right?

15 – The Lone Wolf Howls At Midnight

As time marched onward, I noticed the appearance of more of the werewolves in Magnus' court. I could have passed it off as something that I wasn't familiar with, except that Clio and Gabby spent as much time gawking at them as I did. Apparently they didn't often come into the city. I watched and wondered, unsure what was going on. It was all fascinating, but also distracting.

I was in the Mageholme library, going through a pile of old papers, when I heard the commotion upstairs. I'm not a shrinking violet, but I'm not stupid, either. I paused at the safe room and armed myself with a small but powerful crossbow and a lovely, fat wooden stake. Not everything was vulnerable to bullets, but even the burliest of assassins of any race was likely to be slowed down by a huge chunk of wood poking out of them. To vampires, in the right spot, it could mean immediate and irreversible death.

I slipped up the back stairs rather than taking the elevator we'd installed. Not everyone knew about the stairs , and they were at the far end of the house, away from where Magnus usually held court. I slipped past what used to be my bedroom, along the hallway, and through the parlor. I edged along the wall approaching the dining room/secondary throne room.

I could smell the werewolf long before I saw him. No matter how many times I was around them, the heavy smell just slayed me. Wet dog times a thousand. How could they pass among humans? I stopped breathing, a handy trait for a vampire, and concealed the crossbow in my long skirts. I entered the room quietly, and saw the sizable, burly fellow bowing hastily before Magnus at the head of the big table.

"You know we do not recognize you as rulers in the city, but my own clan leaders have sent me here. The Grandmother felt you were the one to talk to. I don't know that I agree with her, but I follow her will, as always." He held his meaty hands out to the side in a gesture of peace.

It wasn't the werewolf that caught my eye, though. It was the… ghost? spirit? soul that hovered about him as he stood there. It was a woman, large like himself, muscular, almost masculine in her shape. She was feminine, though, to a fault. She danced around him as if trying to get his attention.

She looked angry, exasperated even. Waving her arms in front of him, she attempted to block his forward progress. He went right through her, of course, souls having no physical reality. For his part, he was aware enough to shudder violently at the sensation. She looked surprised, then taken aback. She whipped around to look at his back as he sat in the chair indicated by Magnus.

I watched her capering about for several minutes. I'm sure I looked like a fool, mouth gaping open. Most souls are not all that aware if newly dead, and almost bored of it if they've been haunting for a while. None were prone to showing up like this, though, as if they were a somewhat faded but still very real, very physical person. I could see through her, but she had a solidity that was unlike anything I'd experienced before. Of course, my experience was a bit limited.

"Alexandra!" Magnus barked, and I jumped. I looked over to see him staring at me, along with most of the people in the room. Clio grimaced, making a very subtle 'be calm' motion with her hand.

"My Prince," I replied, dropping to a graceful curtsy, careful not to expose the crossbow. "May I help you?"

"Yes, this is Rokku, of the Skinwalker tribe of werewolves. They live in the far north. They are suffering with a... haunting," he explained, eying Rokku and myself in turn.

"I can see that," I quipped, and immediately regretted my words. Magnus' eyebrow shot up, and Rokku spun in his chair to face me.

"What is that supposed to mean?" he demanded in a low, growling voice.

I was about to explain the soul flitting about, when she made the connection that I alone could see her. She gave me a pleading look and mimicked zipping her mouth shut. Her face was desperate.

"I… didn't mean anything at all," I lied, badly. I cast about for a way to explain my actions, and managed to lose my grip on the crossbow. It skittered across the floor, loud and obvious, everyone staring at it. I would have blushed, but vampires don't do that.

It stopped at Rokku's feet, and he glared at it, then me. I tried to focus on him, but I was dealing with a sense of terror at his sheer size. I was also processing my confusion about the transparent woman beside him.

"Can you hear me?" she pleaded, her voice clear and bell-like to me and only me. "I need your help!"

How do you answer a dead woman, without alerting everyone else in the room, while a hulking werewolf and your Prince and your lover and your community Elders all gawk at you? Yeah, I don't know either.

Look for more "Taylor, Mage" books, coming soon!

Other books by M. Allyson Szabo:

Blood Stone
Taylor, Mage - Book One

Alexandra Taylor witnessed the brutal murder of her boyfriend at the hands of an insane woman. Her world was upended again the night he came to visit her, very not-dead, but changed forever. Tracking him across the country led her to discover a world of dark intrigue. She discovered she had impressive talents and skills...and that not everyone friendly is a friend.

Longing for Wisdom: The Message of the Maxims
(as Allyson Szabo)

Know yourself. Nothing in excess. Give a pledge and ruin is near. These are the words inscribed on a stele just outside the Temple of Apollo at Delphi. Stunning in their simplicity, these Maxims have survived the test of time. Delving into both the history and the current application of 34 of the Maxims to the creation of personal ethics and morals, Allyson Szabo provides us with a path to personal growth and understanding of the world around us.